lonely planet KIDS

SNACKS
around the
WORLD

Tasty Treats and Fun Eats from Everywhere!

Lonely Planet KIDS

SNACKS around the WORLD

Tasty Treats and Fun Eats from Everywhere!

WRITTEN BY
LISA M. GERRY

ILLUSTRATED BY
TOBY TRIUMPH

SNACKS around the WORLD
CONTENTS

Snack Time Around the World 6

CRUNCHY SNACKS 8
Chip, Chip Hooray! 10
What's Cracking? 12
Crispy Crunchies 14
Snack Spotlight: Vending Machines 16
Belles of the Bars 18
Veg Out! 20
Snack Spotlight: Seaweed 21
So Nutty 22
Pop Til You Drop! 24
Tasty Timeline: Popcorn 26
More Crunchy Munchies 28

CHEWY SNACKS 30
Dough-licious 32
Snack Spotlight: Doughnuts 36
Breads Up! 38
Toast-tacular 42
Say Cheese! 44
Tasty Timeline: Pizza 46
Extras, Extras! Dips, Spreads, and Sauces 48
Rice, Rice Baby! 50
Snack Smorgasbords 52
Yum, Yum Chewing Gum 54
Snack Spotlight: Gum Ban in Singapore 55

SALTY SNACKS **56**
   Fermentation Station 58
   One Potato, Two Potato... 60
   Snack Spotlight: Stadium Food 64
   Well, Fry Not? 66
   It's a Meat Pie Party! 68
   Snack Spotlight: Street Food 70
   Smoked & Dried Meats 72

SWEET SNACKS **74**
   Fruit-Scootin' Boogie 76
   With Fruit to Boot 78
   Snack Spotlight: Hawthorn Berries 79
   Piece of Cake! 80
   Sweet Spreads 82
   Ice Cream Party! 84
   Anatomy of a Snack: Ice Cream Sundae! 88
   Perfect Pastries 90
   Cheers! 94
   Snack Spotlight: South Korean Convenience Shop Drinks 96
   It's Biscuit Time! 98

CONFECTIONERY SNACKS **102**
   Hard Sweets 104
   Lollipop, Lollipop 106
   7 Fun Facts About Sweets 108
   Ooey, Gooey and Very Chewy 110
   Yummy Gummies 112
   Fizzy Pop! 114
   Tasty Timeline: Turkish Delight & Jelly Beans 116
   Sweet Treats 118
   Choc-o-licious 120
   Quirky Confectionery Favourites 122

INDEX **124**
IMAGE CREDITS **126**
CREDITS **128**

SNACK TIME AROUND THE WORLD

Whether you call it a tasty treat, a midday munchie or an afternoon snack, a nibble of something sweet (or salty or savoury) between meals is one of the great delights in life! The food we eat tells an important story about who we are. Our culture, where we live, where we come from – all of that can be shared in the meals and snacks we eat.

When you try a delicious dish from somewhere else in the world, you are doing more than eating food, you are exploring faraway lands and being introduced to the people who live there. So even when you haven't left your home, your taste buds can travel the world.

This map highlights ways in which people in different countries say, 'snack time'.

NORTH AMERICA

MEXICO
'Merienda' ('snack' in Spanish)

SOUTH AMERICA

CHILE
'La Once' ('eleven' in Spanish, this Chilean tea time actually takes place between 5 and 7 p.m.

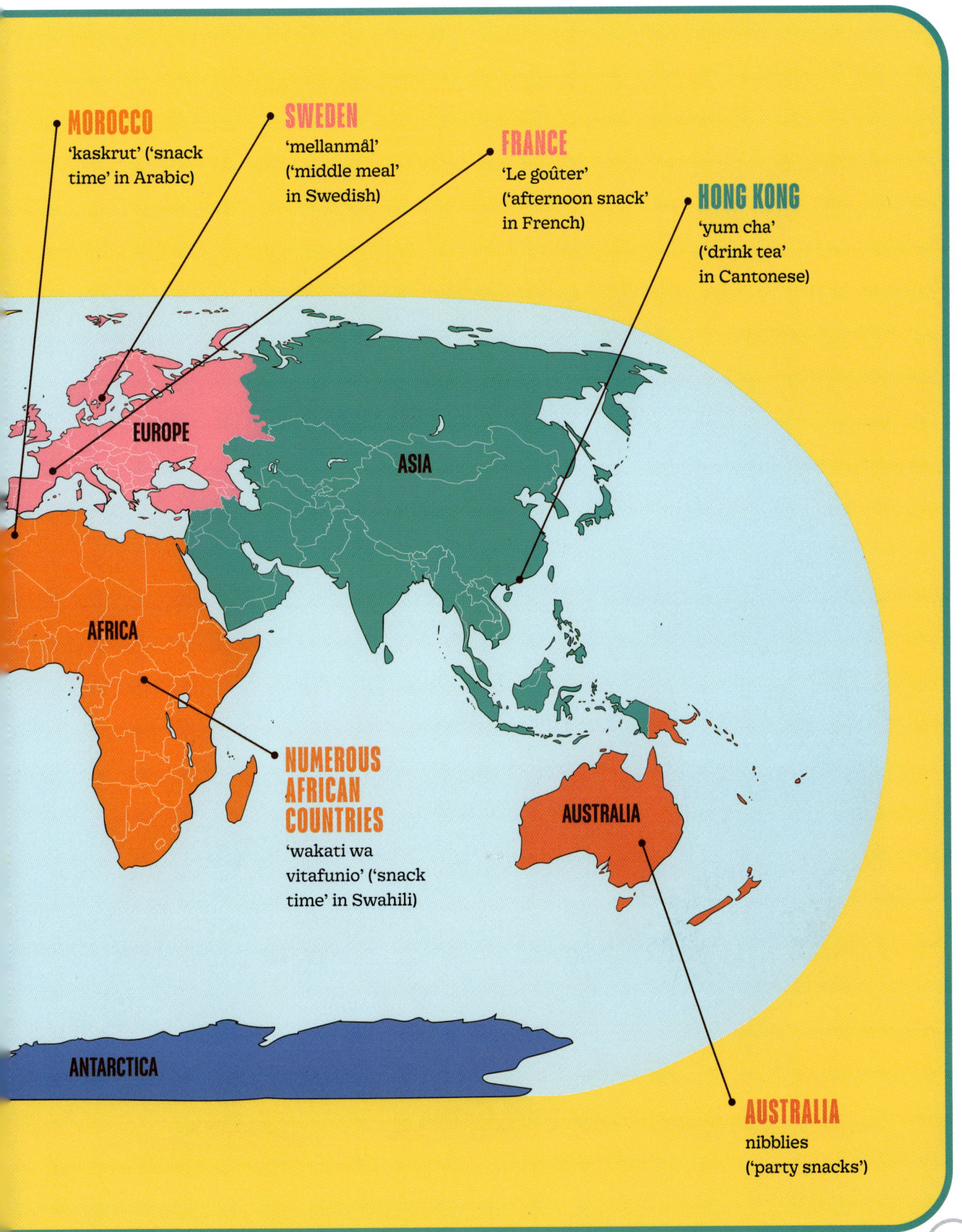

CRUNCHY

SNACKS

Honey Soy Chicken Chip

CHIP, CHIP HOORAY!

You can eat these plain or with dip, pour them straight from the bag into your mouth or even layer them in your favourite sandwich. Fried, paper-thin slices of potatoes, known as 'chips' or 'crisps', are thought to have originated in the United States in the 1850s. Today, however, these crispy, crunchy snacks are enjoyed all around the world. Check out these far-out flavours from across the globe.

Honey Butter
SOUTH KOREA

These popular crisps are more sweet than salty, and they are such a hot item in South Korea that they often sell out within just a few hours of hitting the shelves.

Pickle
UNITED STATES

While flavours such as barbecue or sour cream and onion are favourites in the United States, this slightly sour and totally tangy flavour is taking the country by storm.

Hot Chilli Squid
THAILAND

Dried squid, which is often seasoned with garlic or curry, is a crunchy, beloved snack in Thailand. These aromatic crisps are chock-full of that seafood flavour.

Prawn Cocktail
UNITED KINGDOM
If this snack seems a little fishy, here's why: these popular crisps are tangy and slightly sweet and have a subtle seafood flavour.

Ketchup
CANADA
Potatoes and ketchup are a pretty perfect pairing. Just think: crispy chips dipped in sweet tomato sauce! It's no surprise, then, that this crisp flavour is one of Canada's most popular.

Salt & Seaweed
JAPAN
Japan is an island country surrounded by the sea, and one of its most popular food ingredients is the nutritious and delicious marine plant, seaweed!

Honey Soy Chicken
AUSTRALIA
This popular flavour combines the sweetness of honey, the saltiness of soy sauce and the savoury seasoning of chicken. It's a party for the taste buds.

Chutney
SOUTH AFRICA
Chutney, a popular condiment in South Africa, is made from dried fruits that are cooked slowly with sugar, vinegar and spices, giving these tasty crisps that telltale tangy flavour!

WHAT'S CRACKING?

They're crispy, they're crunchy – they're crackers! These tasty treats are perfect for holding your favourite dips, spreads and cheeses, and they are just as fun to eat all on their own.

Dante Crackers

Dante Crackers
CUBA

These beloved crackers are thick and crispy and have a powdery texture. They're often eaten topped with butter, guava paste and jam, and are sometimes even dipped in a hot drink.

Senbei
JAPAN

These popular rice crackers come in a variety of shapes and sizes and can be baked or deep-fried. They're often brushed with soy sauce and have a salty and slightly sweet taste.

Papadum
INDIA

These deep-fried crackers made of rice or chickpeas are light and crispy. In India, papadum are served with salad, soup, or a main meal – diners can break and sprinkle them on top for a crunch.

Knäckebröd
SWEDEN

The dimples in these hard, dry and oh-so-crispy crackers make them the perfect paring with dips, spreads, meats and cheeses. Yum!

Jumpy's
AUSTRALIA

These crackers will put some spring in your step – they're shaped like kangaroos! They are perfect for snacking and come in salted, salt and vinegar, and chicken flavours.

Shrimp Crackers
INDONESIA

These crispy, shrimp-flavoured rice crackers are not only fun to eat on their own, but also pair perfectly with rice or a meal to add texture and crunch.

Cream Crackers
UNITED KINGDOM & IRELAND

The perfect platform, these thick, crispy crackers are often served with cheese, butter or other savoury spreads, such as the British favourite, Marmite.

BITE-SIZE BACKSTORY
HOW TRISCUITS GOT THEIR NAME

When Triscuit crackers first hit the market in 1903 in the U.S., they were the only food that was made with electricity. The company was so proud of this that they released advertisements touting the fact. That's actually where the name 'Triscuit' came from. Triscuit is a portmanteau (a word that combines two other words) of the words 'electricity' and 'biscuit'. Electricity + Biscuit = Triscuit.

CRUNCHY SNACKS 13

CRISPY CRUNCHIES

When a snack attack strikes, sometimes the only thing that will satisfy it is a treat with a bit of crunch. These snacks all have that in common. They're perfect between meals or as an add-on to something heartier.

Salted Egg Salmon Skin

Rengginang
INDONESIA

These crispy rice cakes are made from sticky rice that is flavoured and then deep-fried. They can taste either savoury (seasoned with garlic and salt) or sweet (coated in coconut sugar).

Velikovi Salt Sticks with Olives
BULGARIA

Sometimes known as 'Bulgarian pretzels', these 'salt sticks' are long, crunchy cracker rods with an olive flavour. They are often snacked on before a meal or served as part of a cheese board.

Koh-Kae Nori Wasabi Flavoured Peanuts
THAILAND

These crispy peanuts come in all sorts of flavours, such as chicken, coffee and coconut cream. The Nori Wasabi mixes together spicy wasabi seasoning and seaweed flavours.

Salted Egg Salmon Skin
SINGAPORE

This snack mixes salted duck egg yolk with crispy salmon skin for a super flavourful – think salty, savoury and spicy – snack!

Fried Fava Beans
PORTUGAL

Fava beans are sometimes called 'broad beans', and are a popular ingredient in Portuguese food. To give this snack the perfect crunch, the beans are peeled and fried.

Simba Ghost Pops
SOUTH AFRICA

There's nothing spooky about these snacks – in fact, they're a fan favourite! The salty corn puffs are full of flavour from ingredients such as onions, tomatoes and spices.

Calbee JagaRico Umami Seaweed
JAPAN

Umami, which has a rich savoury tang, is one of the main five flavours, along with sweet, salty, sour and bitter. These crispy little sticks made from fried potato are swimming in umami seaweed taste.

CRUNCHY SNACKS   15

SNACK SPOTLIGHT
VENDING MACHINES

The very first vending machines appeared in Britain and the United States in the late 1800s, and each dispensed a single item, such as a book of postage stamps, a packet of chewing gum or a bag of peanuts. Shortly after, inventors began creating machines that could also sell a variety of fizzy drinks and other snacks. Fast forward to today and vending machines are everywhere – in schools, office buildings, airports and train stations. And there seems to be no limit to what sweet, savoury – and surprising! – snacks they offer.

Check out these 8 wild and wacky vending machines from around the world!

Canned Breads
JAPAN

From what looks like a simple tin of soup, you can unwrap a loaf of bread, which comes in fun flavours, such as strawberry and chocolate!

Eggs
FRANCE

In France, farmers are turning to countryside vending machines (called *vente en casier*) to sell their goods. Milk, produce, meat and eggs can all be found in vending machines!

Hamburgers
RUSSIA

Choose all the toppings you want and get a hamburger made to order at these vending machines that are found around the world, including at Moscow Airport in Russia.

Cupcakes
UNITED STATES

In 2012, in Beverly Hills, California, Sprinkles Cupcakes launched the world's first cupcake vending machine. As for flavours, they always have the popular red velvet, and they switch between others such as banana, salted caramel and chocolate marshmallow.

Full Hot Meals
SINGAPORE

If you're really hungry on the go, that's no problem in Singapore! Beyond just snacks, diners here can get a full meal, including seafood pasta, chicken curry or lasagna, from Chef-In-Box vending machines.

Bananas
JAPAN

This is *bananas*! There's a whole vending machine devoted to the famous fruit. You can buy one banana for about 150 Yen (US$1), which if you need a quick, healthy pick-me-up, you'll find very a-*peel*-ing!

Baguettes
FRANCE

In France, when the local bakery (called a *boulangerie*) is closed, vending machines ensure that you are never far from the country's signature snack – baguettes. This crusty bread is great with some butter or cheese or just on its own.

Pizzas
ITALY

At the Let's Pizza vending machine, after choosing one of eight different style pizzas, the dough is freshly kneaded and the pizza is made to order in less than three minutes.

17

Melekouni

BELLES OF THE BARS

Not quite a biscuit, and definitely not a cracker, these grab-and-go snack bars combine loads of tasty ingredients.

Gozinaki
GEORGIA

A holiday favourite, Gozinaki is made with caramelised nuts – usually walnuts, hazelnuts or almonds – fried in honey is often served as part of New Year celebrations.

Granola Bars
UNITED STATES

When US snack companies heard about granola bars, they took the idea and ran with it. Today, you can find crunchy ones, chewy ones, some with nuts and fruits, and others with coconut or chocolate! What do they all have in common? Oats are always the main ingredient.

Flapjack
UNITED KINGDOM

At their most basic, these thick snack bars are made from oats, butter, golden syrup and sugar. But, beyond that, the possible add-ins are endless: chocolate, coconut flakes, nuts, dried fruits, seeds and even marmalade – to name a few!

Melekouni
GREECE

Made from sesame seeds, almonds, honey, citrus zest and spices, these chewy bars are a flavour fiesta in your mouth! What makes them even better? All these great ingredients make them healthy, too!

Peanut Drops
JAMAICA

Peanuts, grated ginger and brown sugar are all it takes to create these chewy snacks. They might be made of just a few ingredients, but these little snacks have big-time flavour.

Sachima
CHINA

Pieces of fried dough are mixed with sugar syrup and deep-fried to make these chewy bars. They can then be topped with a sprinkling of sesame seeds, coconut, watermelon seeds or dried fruits!

CRUNCHY SNACKS

VEG OUT!

We know, we know, it's important to eat vegetables! But depending on where you are in the world, the veggies you eat – and how you eat them – might look (and taste!) a little different. Check out these *vegelicious* dishes from across the globe.

Cactus Fry

Green Peas
PHILIPPINES

These crunchy, salty peas are a popular treat and are sold in individual snack bags. They come in an original or spicy beef flavour, or you can buy them with garlic and mixed with nuts.

Veggie Balls
PHILIPPINES

A popular street food, these deep-fried dough balls are filled with a mixture of veggies, such as carrots, potatoes and celery.

Elote
MEXICO

Mexican street corn, or Elote, is one of the most popular street foods in Mexico. The corn on the cob is served on a stick, slathered with Mexican crema (similar to mayo), and topped with cotija cheese and chilli powder.

Takuan
JAPAN

Served with other pickled vegetables as a side dish, or sold in snack packs of three or four, pickled daikon radishes are salty, crunchy and a little bit spicy. And bonus – they're thought to help with digestion!

Artichokes
ITALY
Artichokes grow on thick stalks, and the part that is harvested for food is the flower. In fact, if left on the plant, this part will turn into beautiful purple blooms. In Italy, artichokes are popular snacks served many ways, including grilled, stuffed and fried.

Cactus Fries
UNITED STATES
If you remove the prickly spines from the padded leaves of cacti, you can cook and eat them! These deep-fried slices of cacti are great with seasonings and dip, and they are especially popular in the southwest United States – where many cacti grow!

Crudite
FRANCE
Pronounced 'kroo-duh-tay', this dish is an assortment of whole or sliced raw vegetables. Just think: carrots, radishes, tomatoes and green beans! The vegetables are usually paired with some sort of delicious dip.

SNACK SPOTLIGHT: SEAWEED

Seaweed is a type of algae that grows in the sea, usually tethered by roots to the seafloor. There is evidence that seaweed has been eaten in Asia for thousands of years, but only some types of the marine plant are edible. In South Korea, after someone gives birth to a baby, they are encouraged to eat seaweed soup during the months after to help heal the body and get all the vitamins and minerals they need. As a way to honour the mother and the birth of their child, seaweed soup has become the traditional Korean birthday breakfast.

CRUNCHY SNACKS

SO NUTTY

Pistachio

Humans have been eating nuts for hundreds of thousands of years. But did you know that nuts are fruits? It's true, they are! They're single-seeded fruits that are typically nestled inside an outer casing – for example, shells!

Macadamia Nuts
AUSTRALIA

Macadamia nuts are indigenous to Australia, which means that they naturally grow there (as opposed to having been brought there from somewhere else). Macadamia nuts can be eaten raw or roasted, made into macadamia butter, or used in cooking and baking, such as in a macadamia and golden syrup tart.

Pistachios
ITALY

These nuts are popular in Italy and a favourite flavour in many of their beloved desserts, including gelato (ice cream), chocolate bars, torrones (Italian nougat) and pastries, including croissants.

Karuka Nuts
PAPUA NEW GUINEA

These nuts taste both a bit sweet, like coconuts, and savoury, like walnuts. They are served raw, roasted or smoked. If they're not going to be eaten or cooked right away, they can be dried outside and eaten later.

Gingko Nuts
CHINA

These nuts grow from the Gingko tree, and people either eat them like pistachios, by cracking the thick shells and eating the nut inside, or cooking them and adding them to dishes. They are often served on special occasions, such as Chinese New Year.

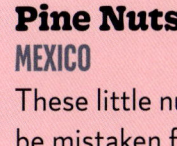

Pine Nuts
MEXICO

These little nuts could possibly be mistaken for seeds and are sometimes described as 'creamy'. They are used in sauces, salsas, rice dishes and more. They're even used in sweets such as pine-nut ice cream and cookies.

Almonds
UNITED STATES

In the United States, almonds are often sold out of the shell, and can be raw or roasted, and served whole, sliced or cut into slivers. They are eaten plain as snacks or are added to desserts, granola, salads, savoury meals, such as almond-crusted chicken, and more.

Brazil Nuts
BRAZIL

The Brazil nut is a large white nut that grows in a thick, dark brown shell on the Brazil nut tree, which is native to the Amazon Rainforest. In Brazil, the nut is eaten raw or roasted, and it can be made into Brazil-nut milk or added to sweets such as ice cream or chocolate.

POP TIL YOU DROP!

Go to any movie theatre in the United States and you're sure to find big buckets of salty, buttery popcorn. But that's just one of the many toppings for this tasty treat. Check out some of the interesting ways people around the world prepare popcorn!

Salted Egg Yolk Popcorn
TAIWAN

If you're looking for an adventurous popcorn flavour, then look no further. This popcorn is packed full of the rich, salty flavour from the yolk of an egg. People who love it can't get enough!

Milk Chocolate Popcorn Bites
ITALY

These truffles are a decadent twist on chocolate-covered popcorn. The 'Salty Crunchy Popcorn' by Sorini have a chocolate outer shell filled with popcorn-flavoured cream and crispy corn. And they're sold in a popcorn-box-shaped package!

Milk Tea Flavoured Popcorn
JAPAN

In Japan, the popular drink Royal Milk Tea is made from black tea, milk and sugar. This popcorn-flavoured version combines the favourite drink with popcorn for a unique, slightly sweet treat.

Sweet Popcorn BRAZIL

In Brazil, popcorn is called 'pipoca', pronounced 'pip-OH-ka'. It is often served sweet, either covered in cocoa powder, sugar or even dulce de leche (a sweet, caramelised milk that makes the perfect topping).

Masala Popcorn INDIA

In Indian cooking, masala means 'a mix of spices'. What spices are used in a masala can vary a bit from dish to dish. The savoury, spicy and sometimes sweet popular popcorn flavour in India might include turmeric, mustard seeds, chilli, garlic, fennel seeds and even dried mango, among other flavourings.

Sugared Popcorn GERMANY

In Germany, it is most common to serve sweet-flavoured popcorn. To make it, the popcorn kernels are covered in sugar water and then popped. You can find this favourite treat at the movies, sports stadiums, Oktoberfest and more!

Lolly Gobble Bliss Bombs AUSTRALIA

If these popcorn snacks don't have the best name, they're definitely in the running! Just try saying it three times fast! Though not as common as they were when they were first released in the 1970s, these caramel popcorn and peanut clusters still have a loyal fan base.

> Not all corn pops! If you try heating up sweet corn from the grocery store, you'll get cooked corn, but not *popped* corn. Only the specific variety of corn known as 'popcorn' will explode into the fluffy snack you know and love.

CRUNCHY SNACKS

TASTY TIMELINE

POP-CORN

Evidence of popcorn was found in a tomb in Peru dating back 3,000 to 6,700 years ago. It's safe to say that people have been enjoying popcorn for a very, *very* long time. Check out these important dates in the history of popcorn.

1612
French colonisers in the Americas meet the Iroquois people who pop popcorn in a piece of pottery with hot sand. Colonial families then begin eating popcorn with sugar and cream in the mornings.

1840s
American colonisers in Williamsburg, Virginia, begin stringing popcorn and hanging it as decorative garlands on Christmas trees. It is thought that this practice first began in Germany.

1885
Chicago, Illinois, candy store owner, Chris Cretors, invents the first machine to pop popcorn. It is steam-powered!

1896
Cracker Jacks, a snack mix made of caramel popcorn and peanuts, hits the scene in the USA. The boxes, however, don't include their trademark toy until 1912.

1929–1939
Popcorn becomes very popular in the United States during the Great Depression, when vendors with pushcarts sell it on the streets for 5 to 10 cents per bag.

Early 1940s
Popcorn becomes the go-to movie theatre snack during World War II, when the United States experiences a sugar shortage and sweets are harder to get hold of.

1950s
Two American companies, E-Z Pop and Jiffy Pop, invent contraptions made of a lightweight aluminium pan with a foil cover that allows people to pop popcorn at home, using the heat of a stove.

1982
Pillsbury releases the first microwavable popcorn, making it easier for people to enjoy freshly popped popcorn at home.

Today, people in the United States eat more than 17 billion quarts of popcorn each year.

27

MORE CRUNCHY MUNCHIES

Food and cultures around the world can be very different, but there is one thing we have in common – a love for a good crunchy snack! These bags of yummy goodies are as unique and full of flavour as the countries they come from.

Carada Cuttlefish Balls
THAILAND

Cuttlefish are sea creatures that are related to squid and octopuses. They are a common dish in Thailand and are often sold by street vendors, either dried or grilled. These crispy, spicy little rice balls boast lots of cuttlefish flavour.

Monster Munch, Roast Beef
UNITED KINGDOM

Don't be scared! These potato crisps are shaped like a monster's paw and come in a variety of flavours, such as roast beef, pickled onion, and 'flamin' hot'.

Przysmak Świętokrzyski
POLAND

These airy, grid-shaped snacks have been a favourite in Poland since the 1980s. Folks buy a bag of them and then fry the treats themselves at home.

Vorontsovskie Rusks
RUSSIA

These little sticks of toasted bread are crispy, spicy snacks that come in different flavours, including barbecue, bacon, onion and jellied meat with horseradish.

Kronchitos
COSTA RICA

These rippled, crunchy corn chips have a sweet barbecue flavour and are beloved by Costa Ricans and visitors alike.

Tako Chips
SOUTH KOREA

These quirky underwater-themed chips have a fabulously fishy flavour. They not only taste like octopuses, but they're shaped like them, too!

KurKure, Naughty Tomato
INDIA

These crunchy little snack sticks are made of rice, lentils and corn, and are packed with sweet, sour and spicy tomato flavours.

CHEWY

SNACKS

DOUGH-LICIOUS

Doughnut

Sure, they come in different shapes, and they have different toppings, but all of these fan-favourite sweet treats have one thing in common – fried dough! When it comes to crowd-pleasing pastries, fried dough is the MVP!

Youtiao
CHINA

These fried dough sticks are sometimes called 'Chinese Fried Dough' or 'Chinese Crullers' and are served at breakfast. They can be peeled apart, used to make a sandwich, or dipped into liquids such as sweetened soy milk.

Doughnut
UNITED STATES

These O-shaped, fried-dough delights come in a wide range of flavours – from sweet (glazed!) to savoury (maple bacon!) to spicy (hello, hot-sauce doughnuts!). They are a favourite breakfast treat in the United States.

Beignet
FRANCE

Beignets, pronounced 'BEN-yays', are pillows of deep-fried dough that are covered in powdered sugar and served hot. They are often paired with chocolate milk or café au lait (coffee with milk).

Poffertjes
NETHERLANDS

Sometimes called 'Dutch Mini Pancakes', these little puffy saucers of dough are most commonly served warm with butter and powdered sugar, and often make an appearance at celebrations such as holidays, weddings and parties.

Bolinhos de Chuva
BRAZIL

These fried balls of dough covered in sugar are known by many different names, including Brazilian Funnel Cake Bites, Brazilian Raindrop Beignets, Brazilian Doughnuts, and even Rain Fritters. No matter their name, one thing's for sure – they're delicious!

Mandazi
UGANDA

Traditionally made with corn flour, mandazi are sometimes served as squares, triangles or balls. They are eaten at breakfast, throughout the day as snacks or at night as a before-bed sweet treat.

MORE DOUGHY DELIGHTS

Kalem Böreği
TURKEY

The name of these fried-dough faves translates in English to 'pencil shape', and they are a bit more savoury than sweet. The thin, crispy dough is stuffed with feta cheese. Sometimes, they are enjoyed as an appetiser. Other times, they're the perfect anytime snack!

Quarkbällchen
GERMANY

The name means 'Quark Balls', which is fitting since these delicious dough balls are made with the German cheese, quark. After they're deep fried, they're covered in powdered sugar, granulated sugar, or a cinnamon and sugar mixture. *Mmm*, how sweet!

Koeksister
SOUTH AFRICA

To make these snacks, strips of dough are braided together, fried, and then dipped in a sugar syrup. It's extra tasty to top them with either cinnamon or lemon juice. These are a popular item sold by street vendors.

34

Kaimati
KENYA

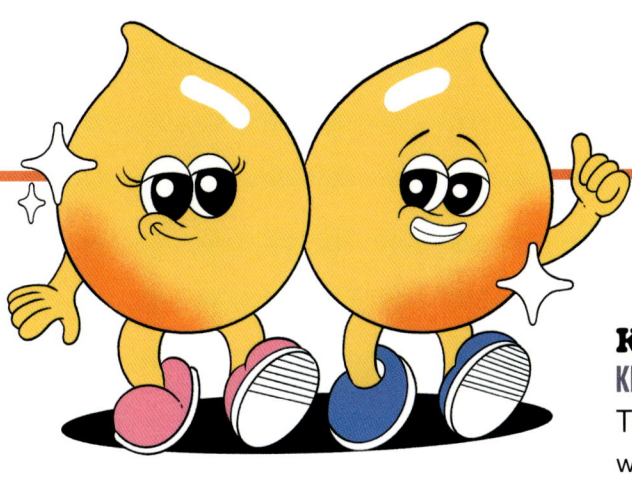

These gooey dumplings are made with yoghurt, fried, and then coated in a sugar syrup with lemon, vanilla and cardamom powder (a spice related to ginger). The special treats are a favourite during the Muslim holy month of Ramadan.

Churros
SPAIN

Sugar-covered, crispy sticks of deep-fried dough for the win! In Spain, they're often served with a side of melted chocolate sauce for dipping. This combo is called 'Churros con Chocolate'.

Tulumba Tatlisi
TURKEY

Pronounced, 'too-LOOM-bah TAHT-luh-suh', these super-sweet short logs of fried dough are beloved in Turkey and are sometimes sold by street vendors. Served in a sugar syrup that is occasionally infused with lemon, they have a hard, crunchy outer layer and a soft inside.

SNACK SPOTLIGHT: DOUGH-NUTS

There is archaeological evidence that doughnuts have been around since ancient times, but it wasn't until 1920 that the first automated doughnut machine was created in New York City, USA. After that, the sweet circles of fried dough with the signature hole in the middle became the must-have treat! They were featured at the 1934 World's Fair in Chicago, served to U.S. soldiers fighting in World Wars I and II, and soon after, were popping up all around the country. Today, doughnuts are beloved internationally and come in all sorts of flavours – from traditional to far out. Here are just a few creations from around the world.

Red Velvet
DOUGHNUT TIME, LONDON, ENGLAND

Familiar flavours like red velvet with cream cheese icing and the 'OG' glazed are favourites here. But so are the unique Robert De N'Oreo and Kylie Mint-Ogue!

The Purple Pig
THE DOUGHNUTTERY, NEW YORK CITY, USA

Specializing in mini doughnuts, this shop still found a way to fit a whole meal's worth of flavours in one – maple, bacon and purple potato.

The Ring of Fire
VOODOO DOUGHNUT, OREGON, USA

This devil's food cake doughnut is covered in cinnamon sugar and spicy cayenne pepper and then topped with a dried red chilli pepper.

Earl Grey Tea and Biscuit
BENEDICT: ALL ABOUT BREAKFAST, BERLIN, GERMANY

With Earl-Grey-tea-flavoured custard inside and a biscuit (cookie) on top, this glazed doughnut is best eaten with pinkies out.

Nerd Party
DOUGHHEADS, NEW SOUTH WALES, AUSTRALIA

This super-sweet, super-pink doughnut is dipped in bright icing made with Red Ripperz, a raspberry chewy candy, and then dipped in Nerds, colourful pebble-like mini candies.

Raspberry Rose
DROP BY DOUGH, BANGKOK, THAILAND

These glazed doughnuts are cake-based and cooked in individual doughnut pans. Raspberry fills the inside and real rose petals pieces are sprinkled on top.

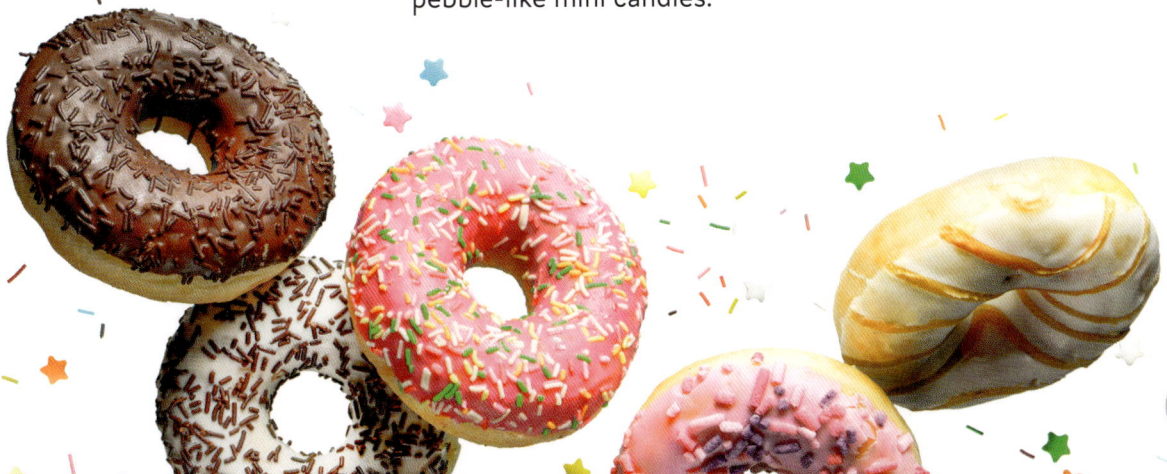

BREADS UP!

Bread baskets, bread sticks, bread bowls – no matter the form, for bread-lovers, bread makes every meal or snack better. Cultures around the world have unique takes on this scrumptious, chewy staple.

Bolani

Naan, India
A light, fluffy bread with bubbles on top and a chewy, stretchy texture
GOES WELL WITH:
Meals such as soups, stews and curries

Baguette, France
A long, thin loaf with a crispy, crunchy outer crust
GOES WELL WITH:
Butter, cheese, chocolate, jam or ham

Bolani, Afghanistan
Fried flatbread with a variety of fillings, typically a mixture of potatoes, coriander and green peppers
GOES WELL WITH:
Yoghurt-based sauces, spicy chutneys or a cup of hot tea

Injera, Ethiopia
A fermented flatbread with a spongy, pancake-like texture

GOES WELL WITH:
Breakfast, lunch, and dinner! Injera is used to scoop up whatever foods you're eating.

Lavash, Armenia
Larger and thinner than pitta, lavash is a chewy, bubbly flatbread.

GOES WELL WITH:
Cheeses, herbs and leafy greens, or meat; lavash is often used as a wrap with various fillings.

Luchi, Bangladesh
A deep-fried, puffed-up flatbread with a crispy, light exterior.

GOES WELL WITH:
Braised meat, deep-fried aubergine, curried meat or peas, or any other sweet or spicy meals

Shaobing, China
Shaobing from northern China is a flaky, chewy, oblong flatbread with a crispy exterior covered in sesame seeds.

GOES WELL WITH:
Soy milk and tea, soup, or porridge – it is sometimes filled with eggs or meat such as pork belly.

MORE BRILLIANT BREADS

Pupusas, El Salvador
These thick, spongy corn tortillas can be stuffed with a variety of fillings, including pork, refried beans or cheese.

GOES WELL WITH:
Cabbage slaw (called 'curtido') or salsa

Khachapuri, Georgia
A boat-shaped bread filled with butter, eggs and gooey melted cheese. Typically, pieces of the bread are torn from the side and dipped in the centre.

GOES WELL WITH:
Butter

Challah, Israel
This braided bread loaf is often served as part of Jewish holiday celebrations.

GOES WELL WITH:
Dips, spreads, or date honey; challah is also used for sandwiches.

Bammy Bread, Jamaica
This thick, dense flatbread is actually not bread at all. It is made from the root vegetable cassava and is soaked in coconut milk before it's fried, steamed, or baked.

GOES WELL WITH:
Fish dishes, jerk dishes, or Jamaica's national dish: ackee (a fruit) and saltfish

Kare Pan, Japan
Kare pan, or 'curry bread', is a thick, crispy bread roll stuffed with curry paste.

GOES WELL WITH:
Rice or other side dishes, or it's great all on its own

Bagel, United States
Bagels are circular rolls with a hole in the middle, a shiny and thin crispy crust and a soft centre.

GOES WELL WITH:
Butter, cream cheese or lox (cured salmon)

Sopa Paraguaya, Paraguay
A cornbread like no other, these are spongy, thick and cheesy.

GOES WELL WITH:
Red meat, chicken or soup

Bayerische Breze, Germany
A thick Bavarian pretzel, bayerische brezes come with a sprinkling of salt on the top.

GOES WELL WITH:
Butter or cheese

TOAST-TACULAR

There are references to toast all the way back to the 1400s. Though we don't know for sure, toast likely originated with people heating up bread to make it taste better after it had gone stale. Today, toast – in its *many* forms – is a popular snack around the world. Here are some popular toast snacks and toppings!

Vegemite

Skagenröra
SWEDEN
This classic seafood mixture is made from shrimp and creamy mayonnaise, seasoned with dill. It is traditionally served on rye bread toast to make the popular snack 'Toast Skagen'.

Labneh
ARMENIA
Creamy, thick and tangy, labneh is Middle Eastern–style strained yoghurt.

Bunny Chow
SOUTH AFRICA
This hollowed-out chunk of bread is filled with curry, sometimes including vegetables, beans, meat or a combination of ingredients.

Welsh Rarebit
WALES

This is a thick sauce of cheddar cheese, mustard, beer or milk and lots of seasonings, served on toasted bread.

Amlou
MOROCCO

Amlou is a sweet spread made with argan oil, toasted almonds and honey.

Bombay Toast
INDIA

To make this classic snack, thick bread is dipped in a spicy egg mixture – including red onions, coriander, and chillis – and then fried. It's often served with ketchup, sriracha (chilli sauce), or chutney.

Prawn Toast
CHINA

This bread is covered in a gingery, garlicky sauce made with real minced prawns, then coated in sesame seeds and fried.

Roti Bakar
INDONESIA

Roti Bakar is the term for 'toasted bread' in Indonesia, and this popular snack is often served as a sandwich – two pieces of toasted bread with various fillings between them. Popular options include banana, chocolate and cheese; chocolate sprinkles; melted butter and sugar; peanut butter; and kaya, which is a coconut jam.

Vegemite
AUSTRALIA

This very popular spread made from brewer's yeast has a strong salty and savoury taste.

Avocado Toast
UNITED STATES

Smashed avocado, olive oil, lemon juice, salt and red pepper flakes are common toppings on this healthy snack. But people add all sorts of other ingredients, such as tomatoes, salmon, bacon, feta cheese, eggs, herbs, seeds and more!

CHEWY SNACKS

SAY CHEESE!

Cheese is made from milk, usually from cows, goats or sheep. Depending on where you are in the world, different types of cheeses, and different flavours and additional ingredients, will be more common. Here are some beloved cheeses from around the globe.

Chechil

String Cheese
UNITED STATES

This favourite lunch-box snack is thought to have been invented in Wisconsin in the 1970s. Today, kids and adults alike love being able to peel long, bite-size strands from a cheese stick at snack time.

Brie
FRANCE

This soft and creamy cheese has a white outer rind (which is edible) and is often served with crusty baguettes, honey, fruits or fruit preserves. Brie can be served at room temperature, baked or inside puff pastry.

Paneer
INDIA

This soft cheese is a part of many meals in India. It can be cubed, grated, or crumbled, but an interesting fact about paneer is that it doesn't melt. This cheese is often used in curries, salads, stir-fries and even desserts!

Poutine
CANADA

Poutine, which is French fries topped with gravy and cheese curds (small pieces of curdled milk), is a Canadian favourite. The dish is served at diners, sporting events and fast-food restaurants.

Chechil
ARMENIA

This cheese is pulled into long, thin strings and soaked in brine (super-salty water), and then, when it is dry, it's hand braided. Nicknamed 'Armenian string cheese', it is eaten by itself or served on snack platters alongside olives and nuts. It also is a favourite in sandwiches and salads, or on baked dishes such as panrkhash, which is similar to macaroni and cheese.

Halloumi
CYPRUS

Halloumi is often described with a funny and unexpected adjective – squeaky. Because of how it's made, it sometimes squeaks when it rubs against someone's teeth. Halloumi is made of a mixture of sheep's and goat's milk (and sometimes cow's milk, too!). In Cyprus, halloumi is enjoyed raw at breakfast, paired with fruit, fried and added to sandwiches or even grated over pasta.

Fondue
SWITZERLAND

Fondue is more than just a food, it's an experience. A selection of cheeses is melted in a special pot with corn flour or flour, wine, herbs and spices. Diners then use long metal forks to dip food into the gooey cheesy mixture. What to dip? Think cubes of bread, meat, veggies, mushrooms, pretzels, potatoes and more.

BITE-SIZE BACKSTORY FONDUE

Fondue was first described in *The Iliad*, a famous multipart poem thought to have been composed by the ancient Greek poet, Homer, in about 800 B.C.E. He described a dish made from melted goat cheese, flour and wine. But it wasn't until the 1800s, in the Swiss and French Alps, that fondue became popular. It has been said that it was a way for people to use hardened cheeses (by melting them) and old bread (which they dipped in the melted cheese) during the winter months when fresh produce was hard to come by.

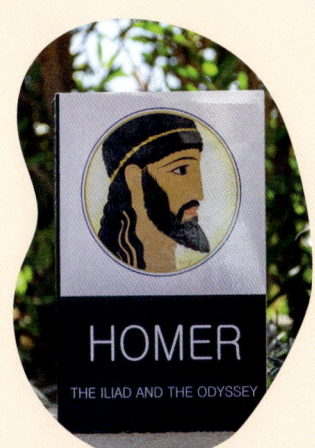

TASTY TIMELINE PIZZA

Today, you can order just about any kind of pizza – breakfast pizza, dessert pizza, seafood pizza, taco pizza or even cheeseburger pizza – the possibilities and toppings are endless! But where did pizza begin, and how did it become the meal- and snack-time superstar that it is today?

1700s and Early 1800s

In Naples, Italy, there is a large population of people who work hard, physically demanding jobs and who have very little money. They need food that is inexpensive and that they can eat quickly. Enter: pizza! The Neapolitans add toppings – much like the ones we eat today – to flatbread and call it a meal!

1889

When Italy's King Umberto I and Queen Margherita of Savoy visit Naples, the legend goes that they grow tired of their fancy food and they ask to try pizza, which they had seen being eaten on the streets. The queen's favourite is one topped with soft white cheese, tomatoes and basil – a combo that since then has been known as 'Pizza Margherita' (or margherita pizza).

Late 1800s and Early 1900s

Immigrants from Naples begin arriving in the United States to begin jobs working in factories, and along with them, they bring pizza. Soon, many others are loving the delicious dish.

1905
The first pizzeria opens in the United States: G. Lombardi's on Spring Street in Manhattan, New York City.

1950s
After World War II, Americans' love of pizza really takes off, and so do frozen pizzas. Restaurants begin selling pizzas that customers can take home and put in their freezer until they are ready to cook and eat them. In years to come, countries around the world import frozen pizzas from the United States to sell in their stores.

1962
Sam Panopoulos, a Greek immigrant, invents the first pineapple-topped 'Hawaiian pizza' in restaurants in Ontario, Canada.

1980
The brand Grandiosa launches its first frozen pizza in Norway, where many citizens have yet to even try the dish. Today, Grandiosa frozen pizza is nicknamed Norway's national dish, and the country is the world's greatest consumer of pizza!

1985
McDonalds sells the first McPizza at a couple of stores in the U.S. In the years that follow, the chain offers McPizza at more stores around the country, but McDonalds officially stops all sales of the pizza in 2017.

1988
Two years before the first fast-food restaurant opens in Russia, the first pizza arrives to the country, served from an Astro Pizza van. Today, a popular style of pizza in Russia is the 'Mockba pizza', topped with sardines, tuna, mackerel, salmon, onions, and herbs.

2023
The Guinness World Record for the largest pizza is set by one measuring 1,297 square metres. It is made with 13,653 pounds of dough, 6,193 kilogrammes of marinara sauce, 3,992 kilogrammes off cheese, and roughly 630,496 pepperoni slices.

UNIQUE TOPPINGS AROUND THE WORLD

SWEDEN: Banana curry
BRAZIL: Green peas
GERMANY: Canned tuna
UNITED KINGDOM: Baked beans
COSTA RICA: Coconut
AUSTRALIA: Crocodile
JAPAN: Oysters

CHEWY SNACKS

EXTRAS, EXTRAS!

DIPS, SPREADS AND SAUCES

Sometimes, the best parts of a snack are the extras, such as the sauces, spreads and dips. Made from delicious and interesting ingredients and bursting with fresh flavour, these are some popular – and yummy – bits and bobs from around the world.

Tahini

Hummus, Lebanon
Blended chickpeas, tahini, lemon juice, garlic and salt, with a drizzle of olive oil on top
GOES WELL WITH:
Pitta bread!

Guacamole, Mexico
Mashed avocado, coriander, onion, jalapeno, lime juice, salt and diced tomato
GOES WELL WITH:
Tortilla chips!

Tahini, Egypt
Tahini paste (which is crushed sesame seeds), lemon juice and garlic
GOES WELL WITH: Falafel!

Tzatziki, Greece
Greek yoghurt, grated cucumber, garlic, olive oil and fresh dill
GOES WELL WITH: Raw veggies!

Ajvar, North Macedonia
Red bell peppers, aubergine, chilli pepper, garlic, olive oil, vinegar, salt and pepper
GOES WELL WITH: Fresh bread!

Ranch, United States
Mayonnaise, sour cream, buttermilk, garlic, dill, chives and lots of other seasonings
GOES WELL WITH: Salads!

Ssamjang, South Korea
Gochujang (red pepper paste), doenjang (fermented soybean paste), sesame oil, spring onions, garlic, sugar and honey
GOES WELL WITH: Korean barbecue!

Fritz Salsa de Maiz, Venezuela
A sauce made of corn, seasonings and more
GOES WELL WITH: Hot dogs!

RICE, RICE BABY!

Rice is a starchy grain that grows on long leaves of grass. Most rice actually grows underwater in flooded fields called paddies. To eat it, rice can either be boiled, or it can be ground up and made into flour. Rice is grown on every continent except Antarctica, and for much of the world's population, it is a huge part of the daily diet. Here are just some of the ways rice is prepared and eaten from place to place.

Onigiri

Onigiri
JAPAN

These mounds of rice are wrapped in dried seaweed known as 'nori'. They are stuffed with fillings, including salmon, vegetables, pork, kimchi (fermented vegetables) or mushrooms. This popular snack is sold in restaurants, parks and convenience shops.

Arancini
ITALY

Arancini are usually sold in one of two shapes – balls or cones. They are deep-fried rice balls, usually with something delicious at their centre, such as meaty tomato sauce, mozzarella, green peas, or prosciutto. They're often sold with a side of marinara (a herby tomato sauce) for dipping.

Tahdig
IRAN

Tahdig means 'bottom of the pot', which is fitting, as this rice dish has a crispy top layer that was fried at the bottom of the pot, while the bottom layer is soft and steamed. Spices such as turmeric and saffron can be added, as well as bread, potatoes, pistachios, dried cherries or yoghurt.

Alaisa Fa'apopo SAMOA
Samoa is an island country in the central-south Pacific Ocean where there are lots and lots of coconuts. Many of the dishes eaten there include coconut. This popular snack is made with rice that is cooked in coconut milk and is often served alongside Koko Samoa, Samoan hot chocolate.

Samgak Kimbap SOUTH KOREA
Kimbap is sometimes called Korean sushi, and Samgak Kimbap is shaped like a triangle. Seasoned rice is covered in seaweed and all sorts of ingredients can be added inside, including sliced meat or fish, spinach, eggs and cucumbers. This is the go-to convenience shop snack.

Ketupat INDONESIA
These rice cakes are cooked and served in the most interesting package – a woven container made of large leaves. The rice is put inside and then boiled in either water or coconut milk. The rice cakes are often served with curry or topped with peanut sauce.

Bánh Rán VIETNAM
These little balls are made of rice flour and deep-fried. They are covered in sesame seeds and often filled with sweet red bean paste and jasmine flower essence. Bánh rán can also be stuffed with savoury fillings, including minced pork or mushrooms.

Puto PHILIPPINES
These Filipino steamed rice cakes are made from finely ground rice and are typically served as a side dish or eaten alone as a snack. You'll find them in an array of flavours, shapes and bright colours.

CHEWY SNACKS

SNACK SMORGASBORDS

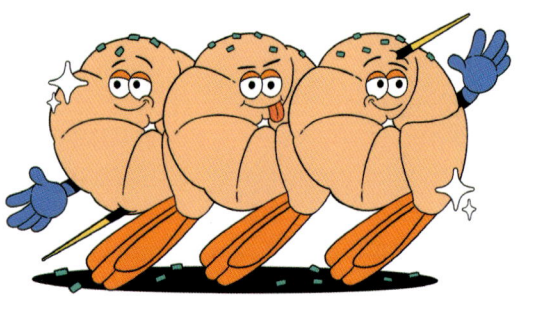

If you're ever in the mood for a little bit of this and a little bit of that and just can't commit to one type of food or flavour, then one of these snack platters might be just what you're craving.

Tapas

Charcuterie
FRANCE

This consists of sliced meats (such as salami, ham and prosciutto), cheeses, nuts, fruits, olives, fruit spreads and bread. Charcuterie boards have become very popular in the United States too, and are often served at parties.

Tapas
SPAIN

Small plates of foods such as dried ham, Spanish omelettes (see p. 61), shrimp in garlic sauce, pork meatballs in tomato sauce, anchovy pastries, mini empanadas, sardines, calamari, roasted potatoes and more

Meze
TURKEY

Small plates of food such as tomato and pepper salad, yoghurt dip, roasted aubergine, hummus, beans (green, broad and Borlotti beans), chickpea and potato pastry and more

Dim Sum
CHINA

Hot tea; dumplings filled with steamed shrimp and/or pork; soup dumplings filled with broth and pork; barbecue pork buns; and various small plates of dishes such as chicken feet, sticky rice chicken lotus wraps, turnip cakes, rice noodle rolls, egg tarts, fried sticky rice balls and more

Tsukemono
JAPAN

Small plates of pickled foods – such as ginger, daikon radishes, Asian plums, eggplant, cucumbers, carrots and seaweed – which are often served with rice

Zakuski
RUSSIA

A smattering of small plates with herring, cured meats, breads, cheeses, liver, pate, caviar, dumplings, pickled vegetables, mushrooms and much more – served with hot tea or fermented milk

Afternoon Tea
UNITED KINGDOM

A light meal served in the afternoon, including hot tea, small sandwiches with fillings such as cheese or salmon, savoury pastries and quiches, scones with clotted cream and strawberry jam, and a variety of small cakes and tarts

Afternoon tea is usually served between 2 pm and 5 pm, and proper etiquette is to stir your tea without clinking the sides of the cup with your spoon.

53

YUM, YUM CHEWING GUM

Chewing gum goes *way* back. In fact, thousands of years ago, ancient people on various continents were collecting substances from trees – such as sap, resin and tar – to chew. In more modern days, in the late 1800s and early 1900s in the United States, a battle for the best bubble gum took place as several companies fought to find the perfect recipe that (1) stayed chewy, (2) had just the right stickiness, and (3) could be blown into bubbles. Today, chewing gum and bubblegum is enjoyed all around the world, in all sorts of sweet, savoury – and even spicy! – flavours.

Bacon Gumball
UNITED STATES

There's an age-old debate about whether bacon is better served chewy or crispy. Well, the debate just got a little more interesting. This bacon-flavoured bubble gum won't exactly freshen your breath, but it will definitely get people talking!

Pepperfruits Gum
JAPAN

On days when you can't quite decide whether you're more in the mood for something sweet or spicy, this one's for you! These little cubes of chewing gum are flavoured with both fruit and peppercorns.

Eucalyptus Gum
GERMANY

You can now try one of koalas' favourite treats – eucalyptus! The brand 'The Taste of Germany' has a 'Forest Flavour' gum that includes the taste of both eucalyptus and menthol. It promises to help you relax while freshening your breath.

Bubbaloo Plátano
MEXICO

Move over cinnamon and peppermint, there's a new flavour in town – and it's bananas! These sugary clouds of bubblegum have even more banana-liciousness in their liquid centre.

Ginseng Gum
SOUTH KOREA

To some people, the taste of ginseng is quite strong and bitter, but others quite like it! Many people consume ginseng for its potential health benefits, such as increased energy.

Passion Fruit Bubble Gum Pops
COLOMBIA

These Bon Bon Bum lollipops have a bubble gum centre and are packed full of the sweet and tart tropical flavours of passion fruit.

Malabar Bubble Mix
FRANCE

This beloved selection of bubble gums contains a variety of flavours, including strawberry, cola, tutti-frutti and lemon-strawberry. And each piece comes wrapped in a temporary tattoo!

> Until the mid-1900s, chewing gum in the United States was made from a substance called chicle, which comes from the sapodilla tree, and was imported from Mexico and Central America.

SNACK SPOTLIGHT: GUM BAN IN SINGAPORE

In 1992, Singapore banned the import and sale of chewing gum. The decision was made after gum was found between the train doors of the country's mass transit systems. Around the same time, public officials began noticing chewing gum litter in public places and venues such as movie theatres. Anyone caught trying to import chewing gum faces a steep fine, or possibly even time in jail!

CHEWY SNACKS

SALTY

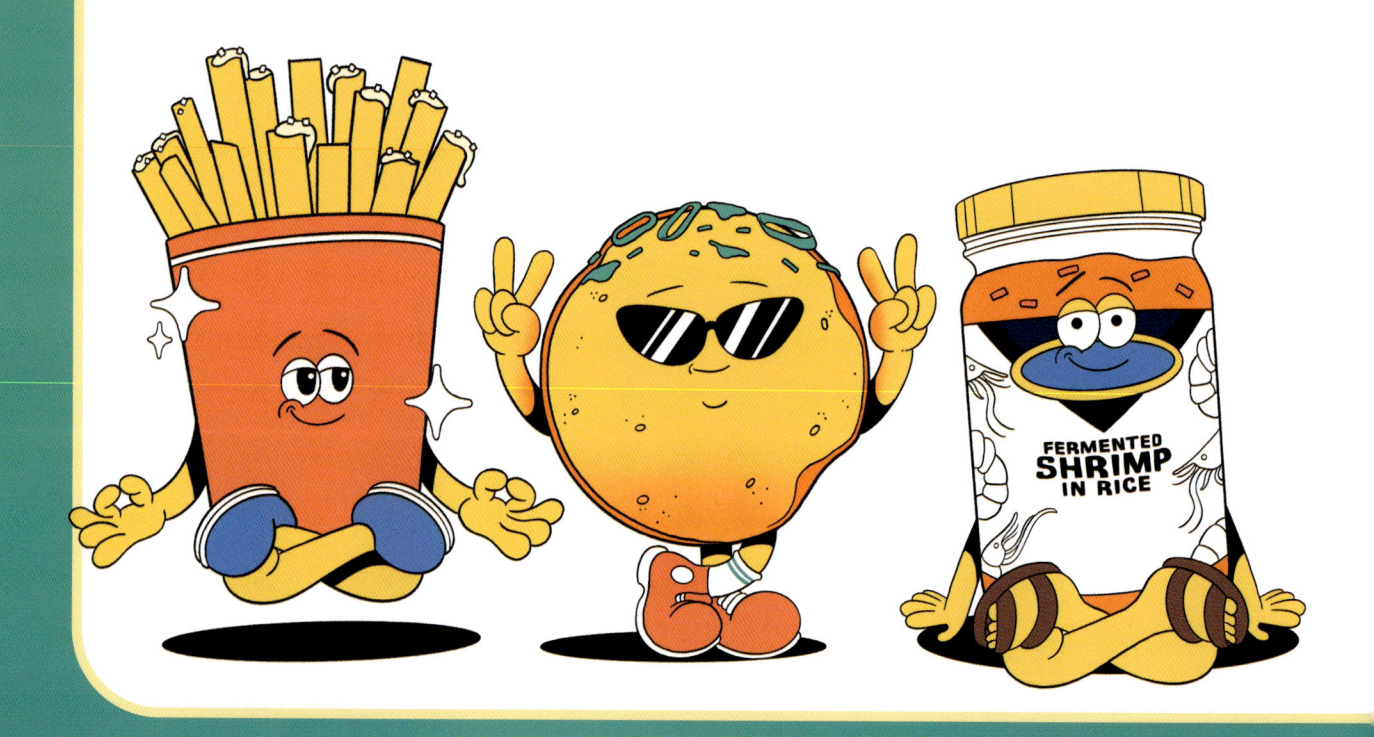

SNACKS

FERMENTATION STATION

Both pickling and fermenting are processes that help foods last longer. To pickle foods, they're added to either vinegar or brine, which is salt water. Fermentation is a chemical reaction that happens to foods thanks to tiny living things called yeasts, bacteria or moulds. Here are some pickled and fermented favourites from all around the world.

Pickle

Pickles (Gherkins) UNITED STATES

Americans love pickles! These versatile veggies can be served on hamburgers, next to sandwiches, in spears, whole – sold from a big jar on the counter of a convenience store and even fried! In fact, each year, Americans eat an average of 20 billion of these tangy, salty, sometimes sweet pickled cucumbers. That's enough to reach from Earth to the Moon and back – more than twice!

Ayran TURKEY

A favourite treat in the warmer months, ayran is a salty fermented yoghurt drink that is served cold. Made of just yoghurt, water and salt, ayran is easy to make and super refreshing. For extra added *oomph*, you can add fruit, mint, cucumber, or even black pepper.

Kimchi
SOUTH KOREA

These pickled vegetables are salty, sweet and sour, and they are a favourite South Korean snack before a meal or as a side dish. Often, kimchi will include cabbage, carrots, radishes, ginger, spring onions, sugar and garlic.

Miso
JAPAN

This super-popular ingredient is fermented soybean paste, and it's used to make everything from soups and dressings to pastas, meat marinades and even desserts, such as brownies.

Burong Hipon
PHILIPPINES

It tastes tangy, salty and totally unique! This thick sauce is made of fermented shrimp and rice, and is used on grilled fish and vegetables, as well as fried fish or in a pitta wrap.

Sauerkraut
GERMANY

This popular side dish and topping is made of fermented cabbage. It's served on sandwiches or bratwurst (a type of German sausage), and it can be eaten hot or cold. On New Year's Day, it's a German tradition to eat pork and sauerkraut for good luck!

Tempeh
INDONESIA

These fermented soybean cakes are a great source of protein. Most people in Indonesia eat tempeh almost daily, alongside tofu, vegetables, rice and seafood. Tempeh can be served all sorts of ways, including fried, steamed and grilled.

Century Eggs
CHINA

Also called '100-Year-Eggs', 'Millennium Eggs' or 'Preserved Eggs', these dark-coloured, jelly-like fermented eggs are considered a Chinese delicacy.

SALTY SNACKS

ONE POTATO, TWO POTATO...

Whether you call them potatoes, taters, or spuds, one thing's for sure – these starchy veggies have celebrity status when it comes to snacks. From chips and fries to tots and hash browns, potatoes certainly are scrumptious shape-shifters.

Tater Tots
UNITED STATES

A popular school-lunch side, stadium snack and sometimes trendy treat, tater tots are a major favourite in the United States. Grated potatoes are formed into small cylinders, fried, and then served plain or covered in toppings such as pulled pork or chilli cheese.

Chipsi Mayai
TANZANIA

In Swahili, this snack's name translates to something like 'fries in eggs', and that's exactly what it is – a French fry omelette! This delicious dish is a popular street food and is often sold with a side of Tanzanian tomato sauce or kachumbari (fresh tomato and onion salad).

Zemiakové Placky
SLOVAKIA

These crispy, pan-fried potato pancakes are often served as a side dish to rich, hearty meals or alone, topped with stew, meat sauce, sauerkraut pork crisps, and more.

Batata Palha
BRAZIL

These crispy, fried slivers of potatoes, also called 'potato sticks', are eaten alone as snacks or used as toppings to add crunch to stews or sandwiches.

Korean Tornado Potatoes
SOUTH KOREA

Originally from South Korea, these wild spud spirals are a favourite snack and street food in several countries around the world. A whole potato is cut into a spiral, put on a skewer, and deep-fried. It's then seasoned with a range of flavours, such as chicken salt, chilli and salt and vinegar. Toppings include bacon, cheese and a variety of sauces.

Tortilla de Patatas
SPAIN

Also called a 'Spanish Omelette', this super-popular dish includes thinly sliced potatoes, eggs and onions, and resembles a small, fluffy cake. Sometimes, it's served between two slices of fresh baguette, which is called a 'bocadillo de tortilla'.

BITE-SIZE BACKSTORY TATER TOTS!

In the 1950s, frozen French fries were a big business. The only problem was that the machines that cut the potatoes into fries left a lot of potato pieces behind. At first, one manufacturer used those scraps to feed his livestock, but then he had a better idea! He formed the leftover potato pieces into small nuggets, fried them, and gave them a new name. And just like that, tater tots were born!

SALTY SNACKS

THREE POTATO, MORE!

Gromperekichelcher
LUXEMBOURG

These thin, crispy potato pancakes are deep-fried and usually served with a tasty dip, such as horseradish or apple sauce.

Crocchè
ITALY

These potato parcels are made from mashed potatoes covered in breadcrumbs and deep-fried. They can be served as an appetiser or as a side dish and are sometimes stuffed with meat or cheese.

Vada Pav
INDIA

These yummy bites of goodness are made by deep-frying balls of mashed potato in chickpea batter. They are often served in white bread rolls and topped with either fried green chillis or a variety of chutneys, which are spicy sauces made of fruits or vegetables.

Kartoffelpuffers
GERMANY

A popular street food, these fried potato pancakes are also used as a side dish for meals eaten at home and served as snacks at Christmas markets. They can be served savoury (with meat or a yoghurt herb sauce) or sweet (with a side of apple sauce or fruit spread).

Pommes de Terre Fondantes
FRANCE

In English, their name translates as 'melting potatoes', and they are usually prepared by cutting a potato into cylinders, browning each end, and then slow cooking them in spices. They turn out very tender and packed full of flavour.

Bulviniai Blynai
LITHUANIA

These beloved potato pancakes are often served on major winter holidays alongside sour cream, apple sauce or jam.

Bajias
KENYA

These deep-fried potato rounds are a deliciously seasoned street food, often served with mango chutney for dipping.

SALTY SNACKS

SNACK SPOTLIGHT: STADIUM FOOD

Whether you're going to watch a sporting event, concert or other live show, stadiums are an exciting way to gather with lots of people to experience something together and be entertained. And bonus – stadiums often have great snacks! Check out a few fun ones from around the globe.

Takoyaki
JAPAN

Takoyaki are balls of battered, fried octopus. They are often served with a variety of sauces, including mayonnaise, and then topped with bonito flakes, which are super-thin fish shavings.

Dippin' Dots
UNITED STATES

These teeny-tiny beads of ice cream are kept frozen in dry ice and sold at stadiums around the USA. They come in flavours such as banana split, birthday cake, chocolate chip cookie dough, cotton candy (candyfloss) and brownie batter.

Sausage Rolls
UNITED KINGDOM

These savoury snacks are made with sausages mixed with seasonings and breadcrumbs, and then wrapped in puff pastry and baked. For dipping, two favourites are tomato ketchup or a tart, sweet, peppery 'brown sauce'.

Sunflower Seeds SPAIN

You can order your 'pipas', as they're called, raw or roasted and salted or plain. Sunflower seeds are such a popular snack choice in Spain that several stadiums have banned them due to the mess the millions of shells make. Other stadiums have begun composting the shells left behind.

Ful Medames EGYPT

This spiced, fava-bean stew is chock-full of spices and is often served inside a pitta.

Chicharrones Chips MEXICO

This snack is actually a type of pasta that you can buy uncooked and prepare at home. Stadiums and street vendors, however, fry the pasta up and sell big bags of the light, crispy snack nicknamed 'pinwheel chips', which you can top with hot sauce and lime.

Bolo de Rolo BRAZIL

This impressive sweet treat is a mega-layer cake roll filled with guava paste and topped with powdered sugar. Some bolo de rolos have up to 20 layers!

Dessert Poutine CANADA

Of course, they serve poutine (fries topped with cheese curds and gravy) at Rogers Centre Stadium in Canada. But they also once served a sweet spoof of the national delicacy – with churros instead of fries, ice cream instead of cheese, and caramel sauce in place of the gravy.

Since 2017, the most popular snack sold at T-Mobile Park in Seattle, Washington, in the United States is 'chapulines.' Toasted grasshoppers! The crunchy little critters are topped with chilli-lime salt seasoning.

WELL, FRY NOT?

Whether they're regular, waffles or curly, chips are pretty delicious just as they are. But add a flavourful topping and they're next level! It turns out that different places dress up their chips in different ways. Check out these tasty tater toppers.

Chili Cheese Fries
UNITED STATES

Toppings: chilli and cheese (extras include jalapenos, tomatoes, sour cream, crushed Fritos (corn crisps), bacon, onions or avocado)

Poutine
CANADA

Toppings: brown gravy and cheese curds

Curry Chips
UNITED KINGDOM

Toppings: sweet and spicy curry sauce

Salchipapas
PERU

Toppings: sausage, ketchup, mayo, and hot peppers

Patatje Oorlog ('War Fries')
NETHERLANDS

Toppings: mayonnaise, peanut sauce, and onions

Chorrillana
CHILE

Toppings: beef, sautéed onions, and fried eggs

Kartofi Sas Sirene
BULGARIA AND UKRAINE

Toppings: sirene cheese (a white, Bulgarian brined cheese)

Khoai Tay Chien
VIETNAM

Toppings: butter and sugar

Slap Chips
SOUTH AFRICA

Toppings: salt and vinegar (extras include tomato sauce and chilli powder)

Masala Chips
KENYA

Toppings: spices such as cumin, cilantro, and turmeric; tomatoes; and onions (extras include chili tomato paste and chilli flakes)

TIME FOR SOME TATER TALK!

In the United States, these rectangular slices of fried potato goodness are called 'fries' or 'French fries', but in the UK and Ireland, Australia, New Zealand and South Africa, they're called 'chips'. In French-speaking countries, they're called 'frites'.

SALTY SNACKS

IT'S A MEAT PIE PARTY!

These savoury snacks pack the punch of a whole meal in one handy-dandy pouch! Meat pies, sometimes called 'hand pies', contain meat, often veggies, and lots of tasty seasonings all stuffed inside a pastry shell.

Beef Patty

Empanada SPAIN
The name 'empanada' comes from the word 'empanar', which in English means 'to wrap in pastry or bread'. Empanada fillings abound, but popular ones include tuna, beef, bacon, chorizo or potato.

Cornish Pasty ENGLAND
This Cornish pastry is a traditional dish of Cornwall, England, and for many, this popular pie is the ultimate comfort food. Filled with minced beef, onion, sliced potatoes and rutabaga swede, locals call this delicious dish by its nickname, 'oggy'.

Beef Patty JAMAICA
The spice turmeric is what gives the crust of these hand pies their signature yellow hue. They are typically stuffed with curried minced beef, though there are other fillings, too, such as seafood, cheese or vegetables.

Meat Pie AUSTRALIA
These mini pies are stuffed with meat (such as minced beef, bacon or chunky steak); gravy; and veggies (such as peas, potatoes and onion). These are then baked in a golden pastry crust. Sometimes, people will top the pie with tomato sauce.

Pastel BRAZIL
One of the most popular foods sold by street vendors in Brazil, pastels are super-crispy fried pouches filled with beef, shredded chicken, prawns or cheese and hearts of palm (a vegetable that comes from deep in the centre of a palm tree).

Pão Com Chouriço PORTUGAL
These delicious yeasted dough rolls are filled with chouriço (pronounced 'shure-REET-zo'), a popular sausage in Portugal. Slits are cut in the top of the rolls, and then they are baked and typically served warm.

Calzone ITALY
The original pizza pockets, calzones are made with homemade pizza dough, formed into a semi-circle pocket and stuffed with pizza toppings such as ricotta and/or mozzarella cheese, meats or veggies. Marinara sauce is usually served on the side for dipping.

Hot Pocket UNITED STATES
These microwavable, prepackaged hand pies first hit the market in 1980 as 'the Tastywich'. Since then, they've been rebranded and renamed, and now they come in lots of flavours – ham and cheddar; buffalo-style chicken; pepperoni pizza; bacon, egg, and cheese; and more!

SALTY SNACKS

SNACK SPOTLIGHT:
STREET FOOD

There is a long, *long* tradition of selling food and snacks in the street. So long, in fact, that street food can be traced back to more than 3,000 years ago in ancient Greece, where there's evidence they sold fried fish in the street. The tradition likely caught on as a way to serve food that was simple and inexpensive to people who didn't have a lot of money.

Since then, all around the globe, delicious on-the-go snacks and full meals have been sold from stalls, carts, trucks and even the backs of bicycles. And in many places, street food is considered to be some of the most authentic, delicious treats a person can eat.

Check out these street food vendors around the world.

1. Bangkok, Thailand
2. Tel Aviv, Israel
3. Paris, France
4. Mexico City, Mexico
5. New York City, United States
6. Tokyo, Japan
7. Marrakesh, Morocco

A BLAST FROM STREET FOOD'S PAST

In 1920, Harry Burt, who owned a confectionery and ice cream store in Ohio, USA, invented a new treat – a bar of vanilla ice cream covered in chocolate. When he gave it to his daughter, her feedback changed the course of ice cream history. She said that while the treat was delicious, it was too messy to eat. Her brother had an idea – what if it had a handle? Like a stick! Just like that, the first ice cream on a stick was born. Harry called it a Good Humor bar. Soon after, he started selling his new ice cream treats out of refrigerated trucks. He added bells to the trucks so that kids could hear them coming. These were the first ice cream trucks in the United States!

The first set of bells Harry Burt used for one of his refrigerated ice cream trucks came from his son's bobsled.

SMOKED & DRIED MEATS

For tens of thousands of years, drying out meat in the sun or with salt has been a go-to way of preserving meat, which otherwise would spoil quickly. And it just so happens that many people find dried or smoked meat delicious! Check out some of these savoury meat snacks!

Beef jerky is out of this world – literally! The salty, protein-packed snack is a favourite among astronauts travelling to space. The tasty treat can last a long time without going bad and doesn't need any preparation.

ITALY
Prosciutto di Parma
cured ham

UNITED STATES
Pepperoni
a type of salami made from cured beef and pork

MEXICO
Carne Seca
dry, cured beef

GREENLAND
Dried Caribou

NORWAY
Klippfisk
dried fish

SOUTH AFRICA
Biltong
cured beef

SOUTH KOREA
Dried Squid

SCOTLAND
Smoked Salmon

SWEET

SNACKS

FRUIT-SCOOTIN' BOOGIE

There is always so much more to discover! Different countries around the world have different trees and plants that grow in their unique habitats. That means there are probably fruits out there that you haven't tried yet – or you might not even know about! Check out a few of these fabulous fruits. Which one would you like to try first?

Star Fruit

Pomelo VIETNAM
These are the largest of all the citrus fruits, and their thick skin can be different colours, including green, yellow or orange. The insides of the fruit vary from white and yellow to blood-orange or pink. The fruit is often used to make juices, smoothies, jams, salads and sauces, or it can be eaten plain, sometimes with just a little salt.

Durian INDONESIA
These prickly fruits can grow to be the size of a football. They have such a strong smell – which has been compared to cheese or rotting onions – that in several countries, they have been banned from public transportation. The taste, however, has been described as custardy with notes of caramel and vanilla. People drink the juice, add the fruit to smoothies, and use it in desserts such as ice cream.

Key Lime UNITED STATES
Actually native to Southeast Asia, these cute, tart little fruits have gained popularity in the Florida Keys – due in part to their beloved namesake dessert, key lime pie!

Dragon Fruit CHINA
This tropical fruit, which is covered in bright pink scales similar to a dragon's spikes, actually grows on cactus plants. Inside, the fruit is red, pink or white, with lots of black seeds. It has a similar texture to a pear or kiwi. In China, it's added to salads, jellies, fried rice and more!

Mangosteen THAILAND
Once you remove the thick, hard outer shell of a mangosteen, you will unveil the white, soft fruit inside. It is the perfect mix of sweet and tart and can be eaten plain, made into juice, or used in curries, salads and desserts.

Star fruit SRI LANKA
These stunning fruits will stand out on any fruit plate. The tart, sweet fruit has a texture similar to a grape and can be sliced and baked into crisps. It can also be used in chutneys, added to fruit salads or smoothies and baked into desserts – such as a star fruit upside-down cake!

Acai BRAZIL
These berries grow on trees that are 15 to 30 metres high. In Brazil, people climb up the trees to cut the berries down with a knife. Once the berries are smashed, their consistency is like a thick liquid. This precious fruit can be eaten almost like a soup, mixed with sugar or tapioca or added to smoothies.

WITH FRUIT TO BOOT

These sweet treats all have one thing in common – they're all made with fruit! Every fruit grows best in a specific climate, so depending on where you are in the world, different fruits might be more common in the snacks there.

Paletas

Fruit Roll-Ups
UNITED STATES

A lunch box favourite, fruit roll-ups are thin, stretchy, fruity snacks rolled into tubes. Depending on what kind of fruit roll-up you choose, these popular treats range from healthy and fresh to more like fruit-flavoured sweets.

Fruit Dumplings
CZECHIA

These dumplings, called 'ovocné knedlíky', have a sweet surprise at their centre – whole fruit! Popular fillings include apricots, strawberries, blueberries or plums. The dumplings are served with melted butter, powdered sugar and sometimes whipped cream.

Sun-Dried Bananas
THAILAND

A popular sweet treat in Thailand are 'kluay-tak', which translates to 'sun-dried banana'. Bananas are peeled and left in the open air to dry. Today, sun-dried bananas are sold dipped in chocolate or with coatings of almonds, strawberries, and even green tea!

Po'e
FRENCH POLYNESIA

Po'e, pronounced 'POH-eh', is similar in consistency to bread pudding and is made with fresh fruit. The most popular version is made from mashed ripe bananas mixed with flour, vanilla and cinnamon. It is served chilled, sometimes in sweet coconut cream.

Paletas
MEXICO

These refreshing frozen ice lollies are made with fresh fruit, such as strawberries, limes or mango. Sometimes, milk is added to make a creamy version of the popular treat, which is sold in stores throughout the country as well as from pushcarts by street vendors.

Avocado Smoothie
BRAZIL

Throughout much of the world, avocados are used in savoury snacks such as avocado toast or guacamole. But, in Brazil, the pitted, pear-shaped fruits are added to sweet treats, including puddings and ice cream. This popular smoothie is made with avocado, milk, sugar and sometimes a little lime.

SNACK SPOTLIGHT: HAWTHORN BERRIES

These tart red berries grow on trees and are a popular ingredient in snacks in China. There are many sweets made from hawthorn berries, including ones shaped like balls or roll-ups. Haw flakes are thin, pink discs, sold in a tube-shaped stack made from the fruit. Both chewy and crumbly, these flakes are a favourite treat in China. And finally, in a TikTok-famous treat called 'Tanghulu', hawthorn berries are served on skewers – like fruit kebabs – and coated in a clear, hard sugar syrup.

SWEET SNACKS

PIECE OF CAKE!

Custard Cake

Cakes scream celebration and fun! But they're not the easiest treat to take on the go. Enter: snack cakes! These small, personal-size sweets are perfect for when you're in the mood for an extra special snack. And the flavours and presentations are as varied as the countries they're from.

Welsh Cakes WALES
These flat, round delights are also called 'bakestones', which is a type of griddle used to cook cakes in Wales. They have a crispy outside and a soft inside, and they're made with cinnamon and currants (similar to raisins but made from a different type of dried grape). Welsh cakes are sprinkled with powdered sugar and ideally served warm.

Cupcakes UNITED STATES
In the United States, there are shops devoted to these personal-size pastries all over the country. With a wide array of flavours and decorations, cupcakes are popular for birthday parties, holidays and other celebrations. With individually packaged ones, such as Hostess cupcakes, you can even take them with you for a sweet snack on the go.

Pandan Cakes PHILIPPINES
Pandanus amaryllifolius is a spiky tropical plant with blade-like leaves. This popular cake is made with the juice from the plant, which is said to taste milky and a little bit like vanilla and hazelnut. The juice is also what gives these spongy, fluffy cakes their bright green colour.

Lotte Happy Promise Custard Cakes SOUTH KOREA

These individually wrapped sponge cakes are filled with custard cream and come in different flavours, including strawberry, white peach and chocolate.

Balconi Trancetto Strawberry Yoghurt Cakes ITALY

These to-go treats have two layers of Italian sponge cake with a layer of strawberry cream in between. They also come in other flavours, including milk cream, cocoa cream, mascarpone cream and apricot cream.

Pasteis de Feijão Brasão Torres PORTUGAL

This Portuguese favourite has a crispy, tart shell filled with a mixture of white bean jam and ground almonds.

Hiyoko JAPAN

The creator of these cute, quirky bird-shaped cakes was the manager of a sweet shop in the city of Iizuko, Japan. The story goes that the idea for 'Hiyoko', which means 'baby chick' in Japanese, came to him in a dream. Today, these dense cakes, filled with a yellow bean paste meant to look like yolk, are beloved all around the world.

Jaffa Cakes UNITED KINGDOM

Created in the 1920s and named for a type of orange called the Jaffa orange, these snack cakes are a favourite in the UK. The base of the cake is a classic sponge cake. The top gets coated in orange marmalade and then coated in chocolate. Today, there are all sorts of new varieties, including raspberry, strawberry, banana and blackcurrant.

SWEET SPREADS

Whether on bread, biscuits, crackers or pretzels, these delicious dips will make just about any snack session a little bit sweeter. But here are some ideas to get you started. Yum!

Nucita Doble Sabor

Nutella
ITALY

Sweetened hazelnut cocoa spread

GREAT WITH:
Ice cream, toast, bananas, pretzels and crepes

Dulce de Leche
LATIN AMERICA

This caramel-like sauce's name means 'sweet [made] of milk' in English.

GREAT WITH:
Toast, waffles, brownies and biscuits, or stirred in hot chocolate

Nucita Doble Sabor
VENEZUELA

A combination of hazelnut chocolate cream and milk cream

GREAT WITH:
Toast, pancakes, waffles and biscuits

Bal Kaymak
TURKEY

Similar to clotted cream, but made from the milk of a water buffalo and covered in honey

GREAT WITH:
Bread and pastries, or stirred in tea

Apple Butter
UNITED STATES

A thick jam made from slow-cooking apples with spices such as cinnamon and nutmeg

GREAT WITH:
Meat, toast, oatmeal, pancakes, cakes and biscuits

Mango Chutney
INDIA

Blended mangoes with sugar, ginger, cinnamon, chilli powder and various other spices

GREAT WITH:
Curries, rice, meat, naan bread and cheese, or in a sandwich

Strawberry Jam
FRANCE

Blended strawberries, sugar, and lemon juice

GREAT WITH:
Baguette, toast, scones, pancakes and cheese

Dulce de Batata con Chocolate
ARGENTINA

Sweet potato jam with chocolate

GREAT WITH:
Cheese, pastries, crackers and biscuits

SWEET SNACKS

ICE CREAM PARTY!

As the old song goes, 'I scream, you scream, we all scream for ice cream!' And can you blame us? It's delicious! In a bowl, in a cup or in a cone – there's no wrong way to enjoy ice cream. It's perfect on a hot summer day, or hey, even on the coldest winter night. Ice cream and other frozen treats know how to bring the fun!

Baobab Ice Cream

Baobab Ice Cream
SOUTHERN AFRICA

The majestic baobab trees in Southern Africa produce a fruit that can be turned into a powder for cooking. The tart, sweet flavour is great on its own in ice cream, and also goes well with other flavours such as caramel, dragon fruit, raspberry or banana.

99 Flake
UNITED KINGDOM

Cadbury has been making chocolate in the UK since the 1800s, and one of their most popular chocolate bars, the Flake, was first dreamt up in 1920. This crumbly, flaky bar is made of thin folds of chocolate. Not long after it hit the market, people began breaking the Flake in half and adding it to an ice cream cone. They called the creamy creation a '99'.

Spaghettieis
GERMANY

This unique ice cream dessert resembles a bowl full of spaghetti! The ice cream is put through a potato ricer to make it look like spaghetti noodles. The 'spaghetti sauce' is actually a strawberry sauce, and as for the 'parmesan cheese crumbles', those are made with white chocolate shavings. Sometimes, a biscuit or wafer is added to look like garlic bread.

Dondurma
TURKEY

Turkey's ice cream has a unique quality that sets it apart from other ice creams around the globe. Not only is it creamy and sweet, this frozen treat is also chewy and stretchy! Thanks to a few added ingredients (such as orchid flour) and the way it is prepared, it can be pulled and twisted like soft, chewy sweets. It's often eaten with a fork and knife!

ESPUMILLA: A DELICIOUS DOPPELGÄNGER
ECUADOR

While this tasty treat might *look* like ice cream, it is in fact a fluffy, foamy meringue, served at room temperature. It's made from egg whites, sugar and fresh fruits, such as guava, lemon, banana or raspberry. Espumilla is served in ice cream cones and often topped with sprinkles, shredded coconut, fresh fruit, or a special syrup made from blackberries.

SWEET SNACKS

MORE FROZEN FAVOURITES

Tiger Tail Ice Cream
CANADA
While it hasn't caught on in other parts of the world just yet, Canadians love this unique ice cream flavour – orange with swirls of black liquorice.

Kulfi
INDIA
This Indian ice cream is known for its cylindrical shape, which comes from the traditional ice cream moulds. With a super-dense, creamy texture, this treat is served on a stick, and comes in a whole host of flavours, including mango, butterscotch, pistachio, almond, saffron and rose.

Ice Cream Sandwich
SINGAPORE
No need for soft chocolate biscuits – in Singapore, an ice cream sandwich quite literally is a sandwich. It's served wrapped in a slice of bread! Many street vendors offer a variety of ice cream flavours, as well as the choice between white bread or a beautiful rainbow-coloured bread.

Ais Kacang
MALAYSIA
A popular treat to buy from street vendors, this shaved ice is decked out with the works! Toppings include (but are not limited to!) sweet red beans, creamed corn, toasted peanuts, sprinkles and cubes of jelly and condensed milk.

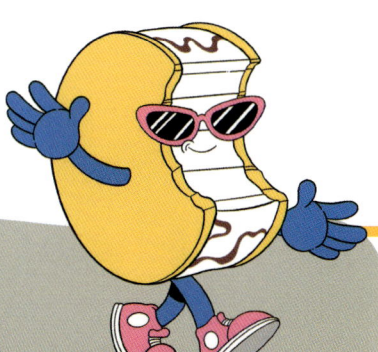

Trits
COSTA RICA

These very popular treats are sold at nearly every convenience shop and supermarket in Costa Rica. When you open the container, you first see a layer of crispy biscuit. When you break through it with your spoon, you'll discover the biscuit is covering a layer of vanilla ice cream with chocolate swirls.

Faloodeh
IRAN

This just may have been the original snow cone. Thought to have originated almost 2,500 years ago, this dish is made from super-thin rice noodles frozen in a syrup of rose water and sugar. Then, a portion is scraped from the frozen mixture and topped with lime juice and sometimes a fruit syrup, such as sweet or sour cherry.

Limber
PUERTO RICO

As the story goes, when the US pilot Charles Lindbergh landed in Puerto Rico in 1928, he was offered this frozen beverage. He enjoyed it so much that they named it after him ('Limber' is a Spanish pronunciation of his last name). Typically frozen in a plastic cup, the mixture is made from coconut milk, tropical juices and sweetener.

Mochi
JAPAN

Boiled or steamed rice is formed into chewy balls, often dyed a bright colour, and then stuffed with an array of fillings, from savoury to sweet to – ice cream! These frozen mochi come in all sorts of flavours, including green tea, black sesame, red bean, mango and strawberry.

Anatomy of a Snack: Ice Cream Sundae!

It's hard to know for sure who invented the ice cream sundae, but one common story is that in the late 1800s in the United States, there was a law that banned the sale of fizzy drinks on Sundays. For one day a week, ice cream parlours needed a new, fun, delicious way to sell ice cream that wasn't the fan-favourite ice-cream float. Instead of pouring fizzy drinks over the ice cream, they used syrups, such as chocolate and cherry, instead! And just like that – *voila!* – ice cream sundaes were born.

Cherry
The quintessential sundae garnish – a cherry on top!

Sprinkles
In the United States, these teeny-tiny, sugary toppings are called either 'sprinkles' or 'jimmies', depending on where you live.

Whipped Cream
Whipped cream has been around since the 16th century and used to be called 'milk snow'.

Syrup
A sundae isn't a sundae without a drizzle of syrup. The flavour, however, is up to you. There's chocolate, butterscotch, cherry, caramel and fudge, to name a few.

Ice Cream
One or more scoops is a must, but by all means, get creative with the flavours!

Other Wild Add-Ons
Crumbled cookies, nuts, gummy worms, chocolate sweets (such as M&Ms), cereals, bananas, brownies, waffles, marshmallows and cotton candy (candy floss) have all been tried.

TO EACH THEIR OWN!

Unconventional sundae toppings include candied bacon, crushed wasabi peas, hot sauce, olive oil, crisps and pickles!

New York City restaurant Serendipity 3 serves a US$1,000 Golden Opulence Sundae. This Guinness World Record holder for most expensive sundae is topped with caviar and edible gold and is served in a US$300 crystal goblet with an 18-karat-gold spoon.

SWEET SNACKS

PERFECT PASTRIES

It's hard to imagine a greater delight than a cake shop filled with dazzling desserts. The colours and textures, the details, and the flavours – these special sweets feel like little moments and bites of bliss. Which one of these would you try first?

Rurki

Bungeoppang
SOUTH KOREA

This fish-shaped bread is filled with sweet red-bean paste.

Bolo Bao
CHINA

These 'pineapple' buns don't actually have pineapple in them. However, when baked, their flaky, crumbly cookie crust topping resembles a pineapple.

Rurki
POLAND

These thin, crispy pastry rolls are filled with sweet whipped cream.

Serabi
INDONESIA

These light pancakes made with rice flour and coconut milk can be served with either sweet or savoury toppings. Sweet ones include sugar, bananas, chocolate sprinkles or even ice cream!

Bolo de Arroz
PORTUGAL

These light and airy Portuguese rice muffins have a tall, cylindrical shape; a lemony flavour; and a golden, sugar-crusted top.

Butterkuchen
GERMANY

Known as 'German Butter Cake', this simple cake is typically topped with butter, vanilla sugar and sliced almonds. It's traditionally cut into rectangles when served and is often enjoyed as an afternoon snack.

MORE BAKED GOODIES

Docinhos
BRAZIL

A must at every birthday party, these Brazilian sweets are made with condensed milk and cream, and they come in all sorts of flavours, including chocolate, coconut and strawberry. They're often decorated with sugar, chopped nuts or sprinkles.

Pastel de Nata
PORTUGAL

This popular Portuguese pastry tart is crispy and flaky on the outside with a creamy and sweet egg custard on the inside.

Mooncake
CHINA

With either a circular or rectangular shape and an intricately designed top, this pastry is perfect for celebrations. Mooncakes are made with many different fillings, such as fruit, black sesame, egg yolk and lotus, red bean or green tea.

Manjū
JAPAN

Like a sweet, little dumpling, this steamed cake is made with different flavoured dough and a variety of cream fillings, including citrus, fruit, red bean, chocolate or vanilla.

Zephyr
RUSSIA

Developed as a way to preserve fruit in the 15th century, this pastry is made from baked fruit puree and egg whites and is sweetened with sugar or honey. The consistency is described as a mix between a marshmallow and meringue.

Kürtőskalács
HUNGARY

These long spirals are nicknamed 'Chimney Cakes' and are made of dough that is covered in melted butter, cinnamon and sugar and then roasted. They can be uncoiled and eaten plain, or they're sometimes filled with ice cream or whipped cream.

Quindim
BRAZIL

This popular Brazilian cake has shiny coconut and egg custard on top and a chewy, macaroon-like coconut crust on the bottom.

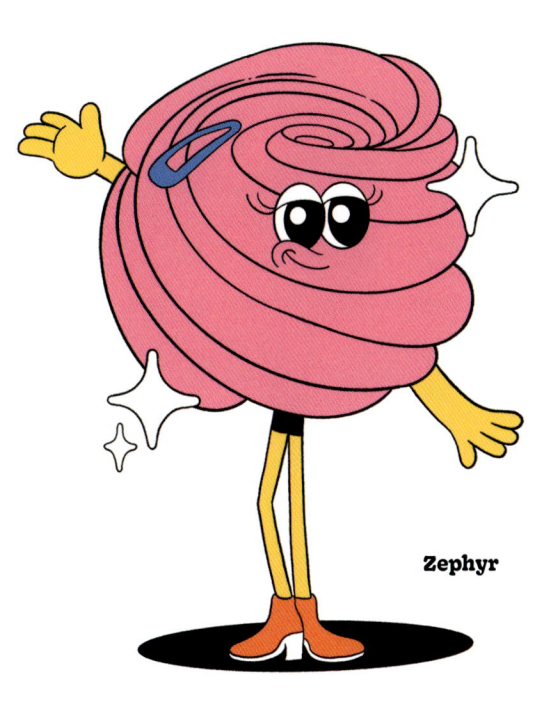

Zephyr

CHEERS!

Refreshing? Check! Delicious? Check! A special sweet treat? Check, check, check! Raise a glass to these yummy drinks!

Bubble Tea

Kefir
RUSSIA

A fermented milk drink (similar to a drinkable, thin yoghurt)

Ramune
JAPAN

This fizzy drink features fruit flavours as well as wilder ones such as wasabi and kimchi. It comes with a marble bottle stopper!

Mango Lassi
INDIA

Made with ripe mangoes, yogurt, cardamom and sometimes a little sugar

Bubble Tea
TAIWAN

A mixture of tea, milk, sugar or flavoured syrup and chewy tapioca pearls called 'boba'

Boba, or tapioca pearls, are made of starches, brown sugar and water!

Eggnog
UNITED KINGDOM

A thick drink made with eggs, milk, cream and spices, such as cinnamon

Limonana
EGYPT

A creamy take on lemonade, made with limes, milk, sugar and mint leaves

Chicha Morada
PERU

A sweet drink made from purple corn, green apples, pineapple, sugar, cinnamon and cloves

Chocolate Santafereño
COLOMBIA

A mix of sweet and savoury, this hot chocolate has dollops of soft white cheese in it.

Banana Milk
SOUTH KOREA

This banana-flavoured milk is sweet, rich and creamy.

SAYING CHEERS

When clinking glasses, friends or family might say, 'Cheers!' Here's how to say it in seven other languages around the world:

Spanish: ¡Salud! (sah-lood)
French: Santé ! (sahn-tay)
German: Prost! (prost)
Italian: Cin cin! (chin chin)
Portuguese: Saúde! (sa-oh-jeh)
Japanese: Kanpai! (kan-pai)
Afrikaans: Gesondheid! (ge-soond-hate)

SWEET SNACKS

SNACK SPOTLIGHT:
SOUTH KOREAN CONVENIENCE SHOP DRINKS

In South Korea, they've found a way to make grabbing a drink at a convenience shop a little more fun. There, right above a freezer full of plastic cups of ice, they sell all kinds of drinks in pouches.

Step 1.
First, you pick your cup of ice. Do you want ice cubes, crushed ice or a cup with just one giant ice sphere?

Step 2.
Next, you choose your drink. They sell a variety of coffee drinks and chocolate milk, peach iced tea, watermelon- or mango-flavoured drinks, blue lemonade, green grape-ade, berry-ade, 'sikhye' (a sweet rice punch often served as a dessert), yuja-cha (tea made from the sweet, tart fruit yuja) and many, many more.

Step 3.
Then, if you want to make your drink creamy, you can choose one of the flavoured milks to add, such as banana, strawberry, melon, lychee and peach, coffee, vanilla or even candy bar.

Step 4.
Lastly, you pay for your items and then mix together your special beverage.

Enjoy!

IT'S BISCUIT TIME!

Crispy or chewy, chocolate chips or chocolate drizzle, with fruit or with nuts – the possibilities are endless when it comes to biscuits! But no matter how you make them, one thing stays the same: they're delicious!

Mbatata

Vaniljekranse
DENMARK
These famous Danish butter biscuits have hints of vanilla and almond flavours and are favourites around the Christmas holiday.

Madeleines
FRANCE
These buttery, bite-size cakes, called madeleines come in a signature shell shape. They have a soft, crumbly consistency.

Mbatata
MALAWI
These soft and delicious sweet-potato biscuits are flavoured with cinnamon and raisins.

Coconut Pirucream
VENEZUELA

Shaped like tubes, these wafers are long, crispy and filled with coconut cream.

Ma'amoul
LEBANON

These shortbread biscuits are filled with dates, walnuts, or pistachio and are a favourite treat during holiday seasons.

Chocolate Chip Cookies
UNITED STATES

There are lots of ways to adapt these classic biscuits, but they are usually made to be either chewy or crispy.

Chocolate Digestives
UNITED KINGDOM

Made from wheat flour, these simple biscuits have one side dipped in chocolate.

Florecitas
PUERTO RICO

Known as 'iced gems' and sometimes sold in metal tins, these bite-size treats come with a dollop of colourful vanilla icing.

Tim Tams
AUSTRALIA

These are a chocolate-lover's dream: two chocolate biscuits with smooth chocolate cream in the middle, covered completely in more chocolate!

MORE COOL COOKIES

Finnish Pinwheels
FINLAND
These have a fun, unique shape and are often filled with prunes or other fruit preserves and sprinkled with powdered sugar.

Polvorones
MEXICO
These buttery, crumbly little 'snowballs' are rolled by hand and always contain some sort of ground nuts, such as pecans, walnuts or almonds.

Macarons
FRANCE
Two round meringue discs are sandwiched together with buttercream, jam or ganache. They come in almost every colour and a wide variety of flavours, including pistachio raspberry and chocolate.

Biberli
SWITZERLAND
This soft gingerbread biscuit is filled with nut paste (usually almond) and spices.

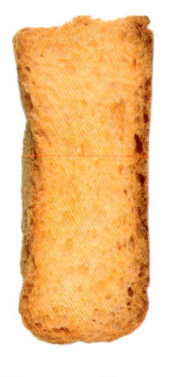

Milk Rusks
SOUTH AFRICA
These hard, dry biscuits are made with buttermilk and are perfect for dipping into a warm drink.

Tunnock's Teacakes
SCOTLAND
Round pillows of marshmallow sit on top of these biscuits, all covered in chocolate.

El Paraguitas Milk Caramel and Guava Cookies
COLOMBIA

These super-crispy wafers are filled with guava paste and caramel.

Ful Sudani
SUDAN

These peanut macarons are usually served alongside cinnamon tea.

Alfajores
ARGENTINA

Dulce de leche (see p. 82) is sandwiched between two super-soft biscuits, which are then rolled in coconut. Some are coated in meringue or chocolate.

Whipped Cream Krumkake
NORWAY

This thin, crispy waffle biscuit is rolled into a cone and filled with whipped cream.

Jammie Dodgers
ENGLAND

Two shortbread biscuits are sandwiched together with strawberry or raspberry jam, with a signature heart-shaped cutout in the top biscuit.

Lebkuchen
GERMANY

Often eaten during winter holiday celebrations, these soft biscuits are spiced with honey, cinnamon, ginger and more.

CONFECTIONERY

SNACKS

HARD SWEETS

Though it might be tempting, hard sweets aren't meant to be chomped on or chewed. Let these sweets dissolve in your mouth as you savour the delicious – and wildly different! – flavours.

Tsitron

Tsitron
UKRAINE
Flavours: a tart and tangy citrus centre with a creamy chocolate coating

Krinos Ouzo
GREECE
Flavours: filled with the flavour of the country's popular sweet and tangy black liquorice liqueur

Gicopa Melon Candy
BELGIUM

Flavours: honeydew, and cantaloupe and honey

X.O. Lemon Iced Tea Candy
THAILAND

Flavours: sweet and tangy lemon iced tea

Matgouel Korean Traditional Scorched Rice Flavour Candy
SOUTH KOREA

Flavours: the toasty, sweet flavour of scorched rice

Motiv Zuckerl
AUSTRIA

Flavours: a variety, including pineapple, orange, watermelon, berry and more

Jolly Ranchers
UNITED STATES

Flavours: green apple, cherry, grape, blue raspberry, and watermelon (original flavours)

BonBon Rådne Fisk
DENMARK

Flavours: salty liquorice and strawberry (despite that, the name translates to 'rotten fish' in English)

> In the centre of the colourful 'motiv zuckerl' sweets are pretty depictions of fruit, including bold orange slices, perfect strawberries and intricate pineapples.

CONFECTIONERY SNACKS

LOLLIPOP, LOLLIPOP

Who doesn't love lollipops? Well, maybe dentists. But for almost everyone else, lollipops are a surefire way to up the fun! Check out some of the ones that kids (and adults!) eat around the world.

Chupa Chups
SPAIN

Flavours: more than 100, including strawberry, orange, lemon, strawberry and cream, chocolate and vanilla, coffee and cream and mint

Vero Mango
MEXICO

Flavours: a sweet mango-flavoured lollipop covered in spicy, salty chilli-flavoured powder

Pierrot Gourmand
FRANCE

Flavours: caramel, lemon, peach and grenadine (a French syrup made of pomegranate, lemon and sugar)

Yogueta Pops
SOUTH AFRICA

Flavours: yoghurt lollipops with flavours such as strawberry, pineapple, orange and banana split

Nimm2 Lizaki
GERMANY

Flavours: orange-lemon, apple-lime, blackberry-blackcurrant and cherry-raspberry

Dip Dab
UNITED KINGDOM

Flavours: strawberry lollipop with lemon sherbet dip

Tiger Pops
COLOMBIA

Flavours: strawberry ice cream, watermelon, cherry, orange, strawberry and more

Look-o-Look Liquorice Lollipops
NETHERLANDS

Flavours: liquorice with a salty powder filling

Melody Pop
CANADA

Flavours: strawberry, blue raspberry and watermelon (it has a working whistle, too!)

7 FUN FACTS ABOUT SWEETS

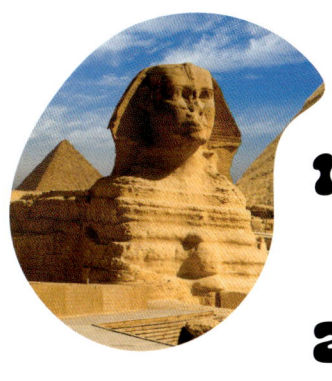

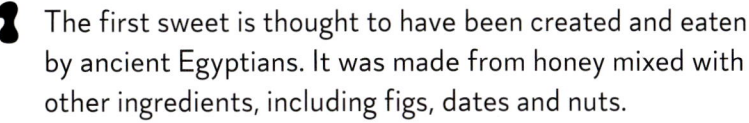

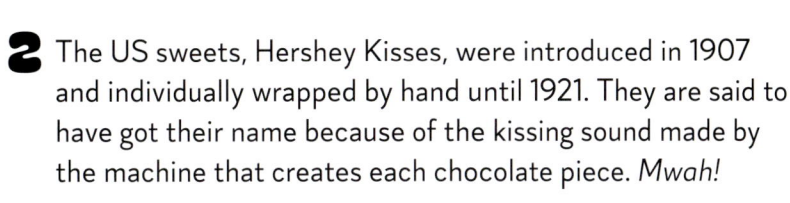

1. The first sweet is thought to have been created and eaten by ancient Egyptians. It was made from honey mixed with other ingredients, including figs, dates and nuts.

2. The US sweets, Hershey Kisses, were introduced in 1907 and individually wrapped by hand until 1921. They are said to have got their name because of the kissing sound made by the machine that creates each chocolate piece. *Mwah!*

3. The logo for Chupa Chups was designed by the Spanish surrealist artist Salvador Dali.

4. The first gummy bear was made in Germany in the 1920s by sweet-maker Hans Riegel, who went on to start the Haribo confectionery company. It got its name from a combination of its founder's name, Ha(ns), Ri(egel), and the city where it was founded: Bo(nn). He named his creations 'Tanzbären', which translates as 'dancing bears'.

5. Chocolate comes from the seeds found inside the long, cucumber-shaped fruit pods of cacao trees. Cacao trees grow in warm places, such as Mexico and Central and South America.

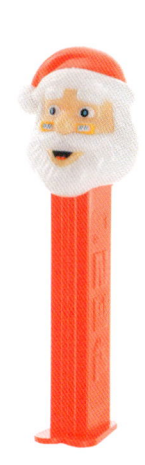

6. Austrian sweet-maker Eduard Haas III invented PEZ sweets in the 1920s to help people freshen their breath and cut back on smoking. When it came time to name his then peppermint-flavoured sweets, he took the first, middle and last letters from the German word for peppermint, 'pfefferminz' – PEZ! In 1955, the first character-shaped dispensers hit the market – a robot and Santa Claus.

7. In Canada, a sweet treat called 'tire d'érable' (maple taffy) is made by pouring a line of maple syrup onto fresh, clean snow. A popsicle stick is then placed at the bottom of the line of maple syrup and rolled to the top, picking up snow as it goes. The syrup and snow mix together to make a firm texture that melts in your mouth.

OOEY, GOOEY AND VERY CHEWY

From caramels and toffees to nougats and marshmallows, check out these tasty, chewy sweet treats from around the globe.

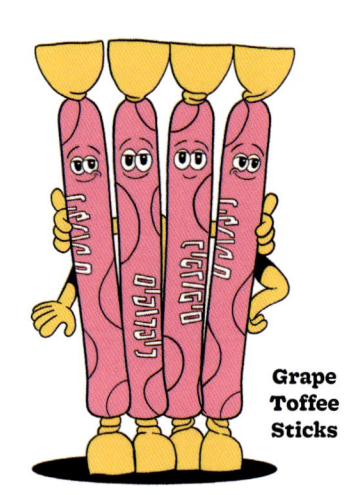

Grape Toffee Sticks

Pistachio Toffees SPAIN
These chewy toffees have the rich, nutty flavour of pistachio cream.

Carambar Caramels FRANCE
These sweet, creamy caramels are a national favourite, and the jokes inside the sweet wrappers are known for being so bad, they're good.

Conos con Cajeta MEXICO
These adorable mini ice cream cones are filled with the Mexican delicacy 'cajeta', a thick, sweet caramel made from goat's milk.

Bon Bons Chewy Candy FRANCE
These little chewy sweets come in a variety of flavours, including apple, watermelon, blue raspberry and strawberry.

Torrone
ITALY
This nutty nougat is an Italian specialty and Christmastime tradition.

Milkita Milk Candy
INDONESIA
These melon-flavoured, chewy sweets have a milky core.

Pineapple Lumps
NEW ZEALAND
These soft, chewy pineapple sweets are covered in chocolate.

Fizzers
SOUTH AFRICA
These soft sweets fizz when you chew them and come in flavours such as cola, strawberry, grape and cream soda.

Grape Toffee Sticks
ISRAEL
These pretty purple toffee sticks have a bold grape flavour.

Jelly Beans
UNITED STATES
A favourite in the United States, these tiny, tasty treats come in more than 100 flavours, including liquorice, cinnamon, strawberry and even buttered popcorn!

Turkish Delight
TURKEY
These sweet, jelly-like squares are often coated in powdered sugar to prevent them from sticking.

CONFECTIONERY SNACKS

YUMMY GUMMIES

Most gummy sweets contain an ingredient called gelatin, which gives them their bendy, pully and chewy feel. Check out these distinctive and delish gummy sweet flavours!

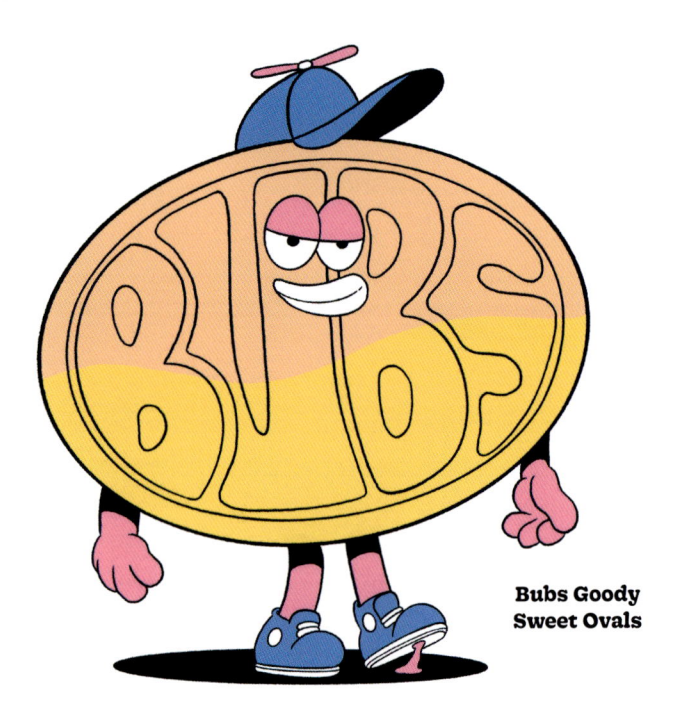

Bubs Goody Sweet Ovals

Julmust and Butterscotch Gummies
SWEDEN

The flavour of Julmust, a soft drink that people drink around Christmastime in Sweden, has been described as a mix between cola and root beer. These gummies taste like Julmust and butterscotch.

Apple & Cinnamon Strudel Gummy Sticks
CZECHIA

Apple strudel has been a beloved dessert in the Czechia for hundreds of years. These treats mix the sweet, fresh taste of apples with the warm taste of cinnamon.

Bubs Goody Sweet Ovals
SWEDEN

These sweets have become super popular around the world thanks to social media. The chewy, foamy sweets have a unique texture and come in strong dual flavours such as creamy caramel, and banana and salty liquorice.

Violet-Flavoured Gummies
BELGIUM

These sugar-covered gummy rounds are infused with the floral taste of violets, a popular flavour in Belgium and France.

Gummi Spicy Mangos
SPAIN

These sweet and spicy chewy gummies have a much-loved flavour combination – chilli and mango.

Gummy Bears
UNITED STATES

While gummy bears were first created in Germany in the 1920s, they have become popular sweets in the United States since they were introduced there country in the 1980s. In fact, Americans spend more than four *billion* dollars a year on gummy sweets.

Yuzu Gummy Candies
JAPAN

These sweet-and-sour sweets taste like a yuzu, a yellow, super-tart citrus fruit that grows mostly in Japan.

Lotte Strawberry Jellycious Gummies
SOUTH KOREA

This popular food brand in South Korea makes everything from cookies and ice cream to drinks and sweets, including these strawberry-flavoured gummies.

> Gelatin, the ingredient that makes some sweets chewy, comes from animal collagen. These days, vegetarian chewy sweets are also available.

CONFECTIONERY SNACKS 113

FIZZY POP!

People all around the world enjoy the fizzy fun of soft drinks. In many countries, popular flavours include variations of cola, cream soda and lemon-lime. Then, there are these more unique tastes to try. Enjoy!

Burst Tropical Banana Soda
HONDURAS
Flavour: banana

Dr. Brown's Cel-Ray
UNITED STATES
Flavour: celery

Mauby Fizz
TRINIDAD AND TOBAGO
Flavour: tree bark

Apfelschorle Carbonated Apple Juice
SWITZERLAND
Flavour: apple

London Essence Co. Elderberry and Hibiscus
UNITED KINGDOM
Flavour: elderberry and hibiscus

Big Bamboo Jamaican Irish Moss Vanilla Drink
JAMAICA
Flavour: seaweed and vanilla

Fanta Banana Yogurt
JAPAN
Flavour: banana yogurt

CONFECTIONERY SNACKS

TASTY TIMELINE

TURKISH DELIGHT & JELLY BEANS

Turkish delight is an eye-catching and delicious sweet treat that hails from the country Turkey. And it turns out that the colourful sweet cubes have served as inspiration for other sugary favourites from around the world, like…drumroll please…jelly beans!

1777
While we don't know for sure, the story goes that the sultan (or leader) of Turkey asks his chefs to make a one-of-a-kind sweet treat. It is then that confectioner Haci Bekir Effendi creates the small, jellied cubes dusted in powdered sugar.

1777
That same year, Effendi opens a confectionery shop called Haci Bekir in Istanbul, Turkey's largest city, which is still open and serving sweets today.

1830s
Known as 'lokum', the jewel-like sweets become all the rage in Turkey. Someone travelling from England brings some home, introducing what he called 'Turkish Delight' to a new country.

Mid-to-late 1800s
The first jelly beans are advertised for sale in the United States, the centres of which are thought to be inspired by Turkish Delight.

Early 1900s
In the United States, general stores and candy stores begin selling individual pieces of 'penny candy' that customers can mix and match and add to a bag. Jelly beans become a popular penny candy.

1960s
Then governor of the US state of California, Ronald Reagan, publicly declares his love for jelly beans and can be seen in photos eating from a large jar during meetings.

1980s
Having become President of the United States, Reagan places a standing order with Jelly Belly of 720 bags per month (306,070 beans).

2023
Jelly beans make their Macy's Thanksgiving Day Parade debut in New York as part of Brach's 'Palace of Sweets' float, which includes holiday favourites such as candy canes, conversation hearts, candy corn, and jelly beans.

Turkish Delight comes in many flavours, including rose water, lemon, mint and apple.

CONFECTIONERY SNACKS

SWEET TREATS

Talk about a sugar rush! There's nothing like a sweet treat to brighten your day, and these special delicacies from around the world will do just that!

Souffle Sweets

Carletti Dark Chocolate Banana Marshmallows
DENMARK

This treat takes a classic flavour combo and turns it into a candy bar! These banana-flavoured marshmallow bars are covered in dark chocolate.

Pomegranate Jelly Candies
GREECE

Pomegranates are a popular fruit used in Greek cooking, and they're considered a symbol of good luck! These sugar-coated jelly cubes are both pleasing to the eye and bursting with pomegranate flavour.

Souffle Sweets
RUSSIA

Souffle candies have a light, airy centre that melts in your mouth. Flavoured with strawberry and dipped in chocolate, they have a slightly jelly-like consistency.

Kuhbonbon
GERMANY

Made with milk, fresh butter and sugar, these individually wrapped soft caramel sweets taste a bit like eggnog (see p. 95).

Pashmak
IRAN

Made from super-thin, pulled strands of flavoured sugar syrup, this delicate, soft dessert comes in an array of colours and flavours, including pistachio, saffron, rose water, orange blossom and sesame.

Marzipan
ITALY

Half sweet, half piece of art, these Italian treats are made from a thick paste of ground almonds and powdered sugar that can be dyed different colours and moulded into intricate shapes, such as little pieces of fruit.

CONFECTIONERY SNACKS

CHOC-O-LICIOUS

Felfort Bananina

The love between humans and chocolate has a long and delicious history. In fact, ancient Maya and Aztec people of Mexico and Central America made a hot chocolate drink from cacao beans, and they cherished the beans so much that they used them as money. For hundreds of years, chocolate was only consumed as a thick drink, but then, in the 1840s, the first 'eating chocolate' was created. And it has been chocolatey bliss ever since!

Violet Crumble
AUSTRALIA

Australia's first chocolate bar, the Violet Crumble was created in 1913. It has chocolate on the outside and a crispy, crunchy honeycomb centre.

Kinder Surprise Eggs
ITALY

Inside these milk chocolate eggs is a fun surprise! You can gently squeeze apart the egg to unveil a little plastic capsule with a toy inside.

Felfort Bananina
ARGENTINA

These foil-wrapped chocolates are filled with banana cream.

Brigadeiro BRAZIL
These chocolate, chewy delights are a must-have at Brazilian birthday parties and can be topped with chocolate sprinkles, nuts, coconut and more.

Milka Bubbly GERMANY
Made with milk from the Swiss Alps, these chocolate bars have little pockets of air throughout, giving them a creamy, velvety texture.

Toblerone SWITZERLAND
These world-renowned chocolate bars are made from Swiss chocolate, honey and almond nougat. The triangular shaped bites of chocolate are designed to resemble Switzerland's mountains.

Chocolate Fish NEW ZEALAND
Strawberry-flavoured marshmallows covered in chocolate and shaped like fish, these sweets are often given to kids in New Zealand to celebrate an achievement.

Chocolate is made of cacao beans, like those seen here. Dark chocolate has the most cacao of the three main types of chocolate. Milk chocolate has milk added to a cacao mixture, and white chocolate has no cacao.

Eating chocolate, especially dark chocolate, can cause your brain to release chemicals that may make you feel happy and calm.

CONFECTIONERY SNACKS

QUIRKY CONFECTIONERY FAVOURITES

These treats are serving sweet and sour (and sometimes salty!) with a side of surprising! They might just make you laugh or have you doing a double take!

Salsagheti
MEXICO

This sweet comes with watermelon-flavoured gummy 'noodles', a packet of tamarind-flavoured sauce, and a plastic tray where you can mix the two together.

> Tamarind is a fruit with a sour, citrusy flavour. It's found in tropical parts of the world. Tamarind sauce is usually a mix of sweet and sour flavourings.

Musk Sticks
AUSTRALIA

These colourful sticks of candy are a bit chalky in texture and dissolve easily, but what *will* linger is their strong smell and taste of perfume.

Chicken Bones Candy
CANADA

While no one knows for sure how they got their name, these bright pink, spicy cinnamon sweets are filled with bittersweet chocolate and are a favourite at Christmastime.

Tayto Milk Chocolate Bar With Cheese & Onion Crisps
IRELAND

The Irish snack brand Tayto briefly released a chocolate bar with another popular product inside – cheese and onion potato chips!

Candied Violets
FRANCE

Take a walk on the fancy side with these sweets made from real flower petals! These sugar-covered violets first hit the sweets scene in the 1800s. They can be eaten all on their own or used as decoration for cakes and other pastries.

Ovos Moles
PORTUGAL

These thin, crispy wafers come in several fun shapes. But the biggest surprise is right at their centre – they're filled with raw egg yolk mixed with sugar!

Wagashi
JAPAN

Often enjoyed with green tea, these Japanese sweets are made from bean paste, as well as other ingredients. They come in very colourful, intricate designs, such as flowers, fruits, fish and succulents.

CONFECTIONERY SNACKS

INDEX

A
Afghanistan 38
Apple snacks 83, 112, 115
Argentina 83, 101, 120
Armenia 39, 43, 45
Australia
    Chips 67
    Doughnuts 37
    Fairy Bread 7, 42
    Honey Soy Chicken Crisps 11
    Jumpy's 13
    Korean Tornado Potatoes 61
    Lolly Gobble Bliss Bombs 25
    Macadamia Nuts 22
    Meat Pie 69
    Musk Sticks 122
    Pizza 47
    Tim Tams 99
    Vegemite 7, 42
    Violet Crumble 120
Austria 105
Avocado snacks 42, 48, 66, 79

B
Bacon snacks
    Avocado Toast 42
    Bacon Gumball 54
    Chilli Cheese Fries 66
    Doughnut 32, 37
    Ice Cream Sundae 89
    Korean Tornado Potatoes 61
    Meat Pies 68–69
    Vorontsovskie Rusks 28
Bananas 17, 78, 95, 115, 118
Bangladesh 39
Belgium 7, 105, 113
Biscuits 98–101
Brazil
    Acai 77
    Avocado Smoothie 79
    Batata Palha 61
    Bolinhos de Chuva 33
    Bolo de Rolos 65
    Brazil Nuts 23
    Brigadeiro 121
    Pastel 69
    Pastries 92, 93
    Peanuts 7
    Pizza 47
    Sweet Popcorn 24
Breads 17, 38–41
Bulgaria 14, 67

C
Cakes 80–81
Canada
    Chicken Bones Candy 122
    Dessert Poutine 65
    Ketchup Crisps 7, 11
    Melody Pop 107
    Pizza 47
    Poutine 7, 44, 66
    Snow Candy 109
    Tiger Tail Ice Cream 87
Cheese 44–45
Chile 67
China
    Bolo Bao 90
    Century Eggs 58
    Dim Sum 53
    Dragon Fruit 77
    Eggroll 7
    Gingko Nuts 23
    Hawthorn Berries 79
    Mooncake 92
    Prawn Toast 43
    Sachima 19
    Shaobing 39
    Tanghulu 7, 79
    Youtiao 32
Chips 7, 10–11, 66–67 see also fries
Chocolate snacks
    biscuits 99
    Carletti Dark Chocolate Banana Marshmallows 118
    Chocolate Bars 120–121
    Chocolate origins 109
    Chocolate Popcorn Bites 24
    Chocolate Santafereño 95
    Map 7
Colombia 55, 95, 101, 107
Costa Rica 29, 47, 87
Crackers 12–13
Cuba 12
Cupcakes 17, 80
Crisps 7, 10–11 see also potato chips
Cyprus 45
Czechia 78, 112

D
Denmark 43, 98, 105, 118
Dips 48–49
Doughnuts 32, 36–37
Drinks 94–97

E
Ecuador 7, 85
Eggs
    Century Eggs 58
    Chipsi Mayai 60
    Ovos Moles 123
    Salted Egg Salmon Skin 15
    Salted Egg Yolk Popcorn 24
    Tortilla de Patatas 61
    Vending machines 17
Egypt 7, 49, 65, 95, 109
El Salvador 40
England, see also United Kingdom
    Chips 67
    Cornish Pasty 68
    Cream Crackers 13
    Doughnuts 37
    Eggnog 95
    Flapjack snack bars 19
    Jammie Dodgers 101
    99 Flake 84
Ethiopia 39

F
Finland 100
Fish snacks 15, 73
France
    Baguette 17, 38
    Beignet 33
    Brie 44
    Candied Violets 123
    Charcuterie 52
    Chewy candy 110
    Crudite 21
    Macarons 100
    Madeleines 98
    Malabar Bubble Mix 55
    Pierrot Gourmand 106
    Pommes de Terre Fondantes 63
    Strawberry Jam 83
    Street food 71
    Vending machines 17
French Polynesia 79
Fries 7, 66–67 see also chips
Fruit snacks 76–79

G
Georgia 18, 40
Germany
    Butterkuchen 91
    Doughnuts 37
    Eucalyptus gum 54
    Gummy Bears 7, 109
    Ham & Cheese Corn Puffs 28
    Kartoffelpuffers 63
    Kuhbonbon 118
    Lebkuchen 101
    Milka Bubbly 121
    Nimm2 Lizaki 107
    Pizza 47
    Popcorn 25, 27
    Pretzel 7, 41
    Quarkbällchen 34
    Sauerkraut 59
    Spaghettieis 85
Ghana 43
Greece 19, 49, 104, 118
Greenland 73
Gum 54–55

H
Hand pies 68–69
Honduras 115
Hummus 7, 48
Hungary 93

I
Ice cream 7, 64, 71, 84–89
India
    Bombay Toast 43
    Curry 7
    Kulfi 87
    KurKure, Naughty Tomato 29
    Mango Chutney 83
    Mango Lassi 94
    Masala Popcorn 25
    Naan 38
    Paneer 44
    Papadum 12
    Vada Pav 62
Indonesia
    Durian 76
    Ketupat 51
    Milky Melon Chews 111
    Rengginang 14
    Roti Bakar 43
    Serabi 91
    Shrimp Crackers 13
    Tempeh 59
Iran 50, 86, 119
Ireland 67, 123
Israel 40, 71, 110
Italy
    Arancini 50
    Artichokes 21
    Balconi Trancetto Strawberry Yoghurt Cakes 81
    Bruschetta 43
    Calzone 69
    Crocchè 62
    Kinder Surprise Eggs 120
    Marzipan 119
    Milk Chocolate Popcorn Bites 24
    Nutella 82
    Pistachios 22
    Pizza 7, 17, 46
    Prosciutto di Parma 73
    Torrone 111
    Vending machines 17

J
Jamaica 19, 40, 68, 115
Japan
    Bird-shaped cakes 81
    Calbee Jagarico
    Fizzy drinks 114, 115
    Umami Seaweed 15

Kare Pan 41
Manjū 92
Milk Tea Flavoured Popcorn 25
Miso 59
Mochi 7, 87
Onigiri 50
Pepperfruits Gum 54
Pizza 47
Ramune 94
Seaweed & Salt Crisps 11
Senbei 12
Street food 71
Takoyaki 64
Takuan 20
Tsukemono 53
Vending machines 17
Wagashi 123
Yuzu Gummy Candies 113

K
Kenya 35, 63, 67
Kurdistan 61

L
Lebanon 48, 99
Lithuania 63
Luxembourg 62

M
Malawi 98
Malaysia 86
Map 6–7
Marshmallows 111, 118
Mexico
    Bubbaloo Plátano 55
    Carne Seca 73
    Chicharrones 65
    Conos con Cajeta 110
    Elote 20
    Guacamole 48
    Korean Tornado Potatoes 61
    Paletas 79
    Pine Nuts 23
    Polvorones 100
    Salsagheti 123
    Street food 71
    Taco 7
    Vero Mango 106
Morocco 43, 71

N
Netherlands 33, 66, 107
New Zealand 7, 67, 111, 121
North Macedonia 49
Norway 47, 73, 101
Nuts 7, 14, 19, 22–23

O
Octopuses 29, 64

P
Papua New Guinea 22
Paraguay 41
Pastries 90–93
Peru 7, 26, 66, 95
Philippines 20, 51, 59, 80
Pickle snacks 10, 20, 58
Pineapple 7, 111
Pizza 7, 17, 46–47
Poland 29, 61, 91
Pop 114–115
Popcorn 24–27
Portugal 15, 69, 81, 91, 92, 123
Potato Chips 7, 10–11 see also crisps
Poutine 7, 44, 65, 66
Pretzels 7, 14, 41
Puerto Rico 86, 99

R
Rice 50–51
Russia
    Kefir 94
    Pizza 47
    Souffle Sweets 119
    Vending machines 17
    Vorontsovskie Rusks 28
    Zakuski 53
    Zephyr 93

S
Samoa 51
Sauces 48–49
Scotland 73, 100
Seaweed 11, 15, 21, 50, 115
Singapore 15, 17, 55, 86
Slovakia 60
Smorgasbords 52–53
Soft drinks 114–115
South Africa
    Biltong 65, 73
    Bunny Chow 43
    Chips 67
    Crisps 11
    Fizzers 111
    Koeksister 34
    Milk Rusks 100
    Simba Ghost Pops 15
    Spar-Letta Pine Nut Soft Drink 115
    Yogueta Pops 107
South Korea
    Bungeoppang 90
    Dried Squid 73
    Drinks 95, 96–97
    Ginseng 55
    Honey Butter Crisps 10
    Kimchi 59
    Korean Tornado Potatoes 61
    Lotte Happy Promise Custard Cakes 81
    Lotte Strawberry Jellycious Gummies 113
    Matgouel Korean Traditional Scorched Rice Flavour Candy 105
    Samgak Kimbap 51
    Seaweed soup 21
    Ssamjang 49
    Tako Chips 29
Southern Africa 84
Spain
    Chupa Chups 106, 109
    Churros 35
    Empanada 68
    Gummi Spicy Mangos 113
    Sunflower Seeds 65
    Tapas 52
    Tortilla de Patatas 61
Spreads 48–49, 82–83
Squid, Dried 10, 73
Sri Lanka 77
Stadium food 64–65
Sudan 101
Sweden 12, 42, 47, 112
Sweets 7, 102–113, 122
Switzerland 45, 100, 115

T
Taiwan 7, 24, 94
Tanzania 60
Tater Tots 60, 61
Tea 25, 37, 53, 94
Thailand
    Crunchy munchies 28
    Doughnuts 37
    Hot Chilli Squid Crisps 10
    Koh-Kae Nori Wasabi Flavoured Peanuts 14
    Mangosteen 77
    Street food 71
    Sun-Dried Bananas 78
    X.O. Lemon Iced Tea Candy 105
Timelines 26–27, 46–47, 116–117
Toast 42–43
Trinidad and Tobago 114
Turkey (country)
    Ayran 59
    Bal Kaymak 82
    Cola Marshmallows 111
    Dondurma 85
    Kalem Böreği 34
    Meze 52
    Tulumba Tatlisi 35
    Turkish Delight 111, 116, 117

U
Uganda 33
Ukraine 67, 104
United Kingdom, see also England; Scotland; Wales
    Afternoon Tea 53
    Chocolate Bar 7
    Chocolate Digestive 99
    Curry Chips 66
    Dip Dab 107
    Jaffa Cakes 81
    London Essence Co. Elderberry and Hibiscus 115
    Monster Munch, Roast Beef 29
    Pizza 47
    Prawn Cocktail Crisps 11
    Sausage Roll 64
United States, see also Puerto Rico
    Almonds 23
    Apple Butter 83
    Breads 41, 42
    Cactus Fries 21
    Chapulines 65
    Chewing gum 54, 55
    Chilli Cheese Fries 66
    Chocolate Chip Cookies 99
    Crisps 7, 10
    Cupcakes 80
    Dippin' Dots 64
    Doughnut 32, 36, 37
    Dr. Brown's Cel-Ray 114
    Fries 67
    Fruit Roll-Ups 78
    Granola Bars 18
    Gummy Bears 113
    Hot Pockets 69
    Ice cream sundaes 88–89
    Ice cream trucks 71
    Jelly Beans 111, 117
    Jolly Ranchers 105
    Key Lime 77
    Map 7
    Pepperoni 73
    Pickles 58
    Pizza 46–47
    Popcorn 24, 27
    Ranch dressing 49
    Sour Flush 122
    Street food 71
    String Cheese 44
    Tater Tots 60
    Vending machines 17

V
Vending machines 16–17
Venezuela 49, 83, 99, 119
Vietnam 51, 66, 76

W
Wales 42, 80

IMAGE CREDITS

6-7: Elisa Lara/Getty Images (world map); **10:** danilo pinzon jr./Alamy CapturePB/Shutterstock Prw_99/Shutterstock (potato chips); **11:** Keith Homan/Shutterstock Shawn Konopaski/Shutterstock anythings/Shutterstock Wirestock Creators/Shutterstock Richard van der Spuy/Shutterstock (potato chips) ; **12:** AlasdairJames/Getty Images (papadum) masa44/Shutterstock (senbei) Roland Magnusson/ Shutterstock (knackebrod); **13:** NorthernLand/Shutterstock (kangaroo crackers) Vladimir Mironov/Getty Images (shrimp crackers) Artissara/Shutterstock (cream crackers) dannyc23/ Getty Images (triscuit) S6Wigj/Shutterstock (lightning); **14:** Fosfi Meta/Shutterstock (rengginang) MIGUEL G. SAAVEDRA/Shutterstock (pretzel sticks) warat42/Shutterstock (nori wasabi peanuts); **15:** goh seok thuan/Shutterstock (salted salmon skin) Q15/Shutterstock (fava beans) enchanted_fairy/Shutterstock (potato sticks); **17:** givaga/Shutterstock (burger) Keith Heaton/Shutterstock (baguette vending machine); **18:** Davydenko Yuliia/Shutterstock (gozinaki) Moving Moment/Shutterstock (granola bar); **19:** Moving Moment/Shutterstock (flapjack) tyasindayanti/Shutterstock (peanut bar) Stefan Tomic/Getty Images (sachima) Ermak Oksana/Shutterstock (sesame bar); **20:** Spalnic/Shutterstock (green peas) Pixel-Shot/ Shutterstock (elote corn) Ermak Oksana/Shutterstock (daikon takuan radish) Aleksandar Todorovic/Shutterstock (buchi); **21:** G Allen Penton/Shutterstock (cactus fries) Carey Jaman/ Shutterstock (crudite) Valeriia Anisimovaa/ Shutterstock (artichoke) Zhane Luk/Shutterstock (seaweed); **22:** popovaphoto/Getty Images (macadamia nuts) Magshab/Shutterstock (pistachios); **23:** Hanasaki/ Shutterstock (gingko nuts) Andrii Horulko/Shutterstock (pine nuts) Nataliia K/Shutterstock (almonds) J_K/Shutterstock (brazil nuts); **24:** huePhotography/Getty Images (corn popping) **25:** P Maxwell Photography/Shutterstock (sweet popcorn) asmiphotoshop/Shutterstock (masala) Firn/Shutterstock (popcorn vendor) InFocus/Shutterstock (popcorn); **27:** eurobanks/Shutterstock (corn) masa44/Shutterstock (corn kernel); **28:** enchanted_fairy/Shutterstock (corn snacks) Steve Stock/Alamy (monster munch snack) Sirawish/Shutterstock (corn snack); **29:** rishi07/Shutterstock (rusk) milart/Shutterstock (bacon chips) The Image Party/Shutterstock (tako chips) NIKS ADS/Shutterstock (kurkure snack); **32:** Satsuei_athian/Shutterstock (youtiao) Valengilda/Getty Images (doughnut;) Jupiterimages/Getty Images (tree) Yeti studio/Shutterstock (popcorn) **33:** Tanveer Anjum Towsif/Shutterstock (beignets) Peter Zijlstra/Shutterstock (poffertjes) Milton Buzon/Shutterstock (bolinhos de chuva) AS Foodstudio/Shutterstock (mandazi); **34:** Fabrizio Troiani/Alamy (kalem boregi) A. Zhuravleva/Shutterstock (quarkballchen) Four Oaks/Shutterstock (koeksister); **35:** 279photo Studio/Shutterstock (churros) banu sevim/Shutterstock (tulumba tatlisi); **36:** badmanproduction/Getty Images (doughnuts); **37:** Richard Baker/Getty Images (doughnut time london) Soho A Studio/Shutterstock (doughnuts) Richard Baker/Getty Images (doughnut time london) Houston Chronicle/Hearst Newspapers/Getty Images (voodoo doughnut); **38:** StockImageFactory/Shutterstock (naan) YinYang/Getty Images (baguette) FarzoTastyFood/Shutterstock (bolani); **39:** Milos Ruzicka/Shutterstock (injera) PNH/Shutterstock (lavash) Elizabeth A.Cummings/Shutterstock (luchi) IMAGEMORE Co. Ltd./ Alamy (shaobing); **40:** Guajillo studio/Shutterstock (pupusas) SnapFocus/ Shutterstock (khachapuri) Danilova Janna/Shutterstock (challah) Haldane/Shutterstock (bammy bread); **41:** masa44/Shutterstock (kare pan) AS Foodstudio/Shutterstock (bagel) Julie Lousa/Shutterstock (sopa) George Marcel/Shutterstock (bayerische breze); **42:** MurzikNata/Getty Images (toast skagen) Oksana Mizina/Shutterstock (labneh) Alexandr Milodan/Getty Images (bunny chow curry); **43:** Elena Zajchikova/Shutterstock (prawn toast) 5PH/Shutterstock (avocado toast); **44:** threeart/Getty Images (string cheese) gresei/Shutterstock (brie) Ravsky/Shutterstock (paneer) Dalaifood/Shutterstock (poutine); **45:** Pixel-Shot/Shutterstock (fondue) hamdi bendali/Shutterstock (book); **46:** Angelafoto/Getty Images (pizza); **47:** Susan Liebold/Alamy (g. lombardi's pizzeria) Stockcreations/Shutterstock (hawaiian pizza) EWY Media/Shutterstock (mcdonald's mcpizza) stockcreations/Shutterstock (hawaiian pizza); **48:** ChameleonsEye/Shutterstock (hummus) bonchan/ Getty Images (guacamole); **49:** Moving Moment/Shutterstock (tahini) Ivan Mateev/ Shutterstock (tzatziki) piece_ov_art/Shutterstock (ajvar) frytka/Getty Images (ranch) Bowonpat Sakaew/Shutterstock (ssamjang); **50:** mauhorng/Getty Images (onigiri) Italian Food Production/Shutterstock (arancini) bonchan/Getty Images (tahdig); **51:** SMDSS/ Shutterstock (alaisa fa'apopo) Najmi Arif/Shutterstock (samgak kimbap) tyasindayanti/Shutterstock (ketupat) PorporLing/Shutterstock (banh ran) Efren Mamac/Shutterstock (puto); **52:** Mila Bond/Getty Images (charcuterie) bonchan/Shutterstock (tapas) sveta_zarzamora/Getty Images (meze); **53:** azfotoru/Getty Images (dim sum) Dmitry Rudnik/Shutterstock (zakuski) Yuuji/Getty Images (tsukemono) Magdanatka/Shutterstock (afternoon tea); **54:** J. Helgason/Shutterstock (gumballs) K.Decor/Shutterstock (eucalyptus); **55:** Picture Partners/Shutterstock (bubbaloo platano) chengyuzheng/Getty Images (ginseng) Merrimon Crawford/Shutterstock (lollipop) Kovaleva_Ka/Shutterstock (malabar bubble mix) luca pbl/Shutterstock (sign); **58:** Yeti studio/Shutterstock (pickles) Kritchai7752/Shutterstock (century eggs); **59:** Olga Popova/Shutterstock (kimchi) kariphoto/Shutterstock (miso) Pixel-Shot/Shutterstock (sauerkraut) Edgunn/ Shutterstock (tempeh) etorres/Shutterstock (ayran) Kritchai7752/Shutterstock (century eggs); **60:** pamela_d_mcadams/Getty Images (tater tots) Alexander Mychko/Dreamstime (chipsi mayai) Caftor/ Shutterstock (zemiakove placky); **61:** AmiNiravTank/Shutterstock (tornado potatoes) rodrigobark/Getty Images (batata palha) NataliaZa/Shutterstock (tortilla tapas de patatas) Yeti studio/Shutterstock (potato); **62:** Ildi Papp/Shutterstock (gromperekichelcher) Sergio Amitiv/Getty Images (crocche) mathess/Getty Images (crocche); **63:** Moving Moment/Shutterstock (kartoffelpuffers) Fanfo/Shutterstock (bulviniai blynai) LauriPatterson/Getty Images (pommes de terre fondantes); **64:** Elio Muchroso/Shutterstock (takoyaki) Karolis Kavolelis/Shutterstock (dippin' dots) Paul Cowan/Shutterstock (sausage roll); **65:** Fanfo/Shutterstock (kenyan bajias) Ermak Oksana/Shutterstock (sunflower seeds) Aninka Bongers-Sutherland/Shutterstock (biltong) rontav/Shutterstock (ful medames) Sergio Hayashi/Shutterstock (chicharrones) Ricardo Alves 1975/Shutterstock (bolo de rolo) Gupi de Zavalia/ Shutterstock (dessert poutine) Dina Julayeva/Shutterstock (chapulines); **66:** etorres/ Shutterstock (poutine) larry mcguirk/Shutterstock (curry chips) etorres/Shutterstock (salchipapas) Clover Chin/Shutterstock (patatje oorlog) Larisa Blinova/Shutterstock (chorrillana); **67:** Dede Permana/Shutterstock (slap chips) Sanoop.cp Shutterstock (masala chips) Angelina Dimitrova/Shutterstock (kartofi sas sirene) Larisa Blinova/Shutterstock (chorrillana) Suzanne Tucker/Shutterstock (french fries) HE Photography/Shutterstock (fish and chips sign) MDart10/Shutterstock (belgian frites sign); **68:** Valentina Razumova/ Shutterstock (empanada) Joe Gough/Shutterstock (cornish pastry) sockagphoto/ Shutterstock (beef patty); **69:** Robyn

Mackenzie/Shutterstock (meat pie) Jobz Fotografia/Shutterstock (pastel) tastytravels/Shutterstock (pao com chourico) siamionau pavel/Shutterstock (calzone) Brent Hofacker/500px/Getty Images (hot pocket); **71:** Bettmann/Getty Images (ice cream truck) Ed Freeman/Getty Images (street food Thailand) Alexander Spatari/Getty Images (crepe France) tupungato/Getty Images (falafel tel aviv) Wachiwit/Getty Images (mochi Japan) Wirestock Creators/ Shutterstock (fruit cart mexico) Merten Snijders/Getty Images (hot dog cart ny) Foto by M/Shutterstock (food cart); **72:** GSDesign/Shutterstock (jerky) Pixel-Shot/Shutterstock (beef jerky); **73:** lathuric/Getty Images (prosciutto di parma) Hong Vo/Shutterstock (pepperoni) HandmadePictures/Shutterstock (carne seca) Edward Westmacott/Shutterstock (biltong) key05/Getty Images (dried squid) MarkGillow/Getty Images (smoked salmon) GSDesign/Shutterstock (jerky); **76:** Zeeking/Shutterstock (pomelo) Photoongraphy/Shutterstock (durian); **77:** SherSor/Shutterstock (key lime) valery121283/Getty Images (dragon fruit) Perfectfood/Getty Images (mangosteen) JIANG HONGYAN/Shutterstock (star fruit) New Africa/Shutterstock (acai); **78:** domnitsky/Shutterstock (fruit roll-up) austrian photographer/Shutterstock (fruit dumpling) Boonchuay1970/Shutterstock (sun-dried bananas); **79:** Larisa Blinova/Shutterstock (po'e) Barcin/Getty Images (paletas) mama_mia/Shutterstock (avocado smoothie) PerfectFood/Shutterstock hantao ge/ Shutterstock (hawthorn berries); **80:** Elena Zajchikova/Shutterstock (Welsh cakes) DebbiSmirnoff/Getty Images (cupcake) Bowonpat Sakaew/Shutterstock (pandan); **81:** Keith Homan/Shutterstock (custard cakes) Only Fabrizio/Shutterstock (yogurt cakes) rfranca/Alamy (pasteis de feijão) lydiarei/Shutterstock (hiyoko) mffoto/Shutterstock (jaffa cakes) rfranca/Alamy (pasteis de feijão); **82:** alenkadr/Getty Images (Nutella) pabloborca/ Getty Images (dulce de leche) Esin Deniz/Shutterstock (bal kaymak); **83:** Keith Homan/Shutterstock (nucita doble) letty17/Getty Images (apple butter) MaraZe/ Shutterstock (mango chutney) syan/Getty Images (strawberry jam) lucianospagnolribeiro/Shutterstock (dulce de batata); **84:** wasanajai/Shutterstock (baobab) Amani A/Shutterstock (99 flake); **85:** Westend61/Getty Images (spaghettieis) VladimirGerasimov/Getty Images (dondurma) DANIEL CONSTANTE/ Shutterstock (la espumilla); **86:** alexandra oquendo/Getty Images (limber) bonchan/ Getty Images (faloodeh) YSK1/Shutterstock (ais kacang) wisnupriyono/Shutterstock (ice cream sandwich) Love In My Oven/Shutterstock (tiger tail ice cream) StockImageFactory/Shutterstock (kulfi) wisnupriyono/Shutterstock (ice cream sandwich) YSK1/Shutterstock (ais kacang); **87:** Love In My Oven/Shutterstock (tiger tail ice cream) anusorn2005/Shutterstock (mochi) StockImageFactory/Shutterstock (kulfi) bonchan/Getty Images (faloodeh) alexandra oquendo/Getty Images (limber) anusorn2005/Shutterstock (mochi); **89:** P Maxwell Photography/Shutterstock (ice cream sundae) Patrick McMullan/Getty Images (golden opulence sundae); **90:** NavyBank/Shutterstock (bungeoppang) JIANG HONGYAN/Shutterstock (pineapple bun); **91:** The Picture Pantry/Shutterstock (pastries) Hamed Studio/Shutterstock (serabi) tastytravels/Shutterstock (bolo de arroz) Bjoern Wylezich/Shutterstock (butterkuchen); **92:** WS-Studio/Shutterstock (docinhos) viennetta/Shutterstock (pastel de natna) Picture Partners/Shutterstock (mooncake) SUNG MIN/Shutterstock (manju); **93:** RHJPhtotos/Shutterstock (quindim) Olga Grozina/Shutterstock (kurtoskalacs) Kristi Blokhin/Shutterstock (zephyr); **94:** NataliaPopova/Shutterstock (kefir) Lazhko Svetlana/Shutterstock (mango lassi) Dwihira/Shutterstock (ramune) Breyenn/ Shutterstock (boba tea); **95:** Pixel-Shot/Shutterstock (eggnog) Hashem Issam Alshanableh/Shutterstock (limonana) Christian Vinces/Shutterstock (chicha morada) anamejia18/Getty Images (chocolate santafereño) Korea by Bike/Shutterstock (banana milk) Breslavtsev Oleg/Shutterstock (cheers); **98:** innakreativ/Shutterstock (vanlijekranse) nelea33/Shutterstock (madeleines); **99:** Ayman Hussain/Getty Images (ma'amoul) Sandhikasan/Shutterstock (chocolate chip cookies) Adrian Burke/Getty Images (chocolate digestive) Creatus/Shutterstock (florecitas) Blue Pebble/ Shutterstock (tim tams); **100:** bonchan/Shutterstock (finnish pinwheels) PRUDENCIOALVAREZ/Getty Images (polvorones) Diana Taliun/Shutterstock (macarons) ksena32/Getty Images (biberli) Kiran Nagare/Shutterstock (milk rusks) Pamela Mcadams/Dreamstime (tunnock's teacakes); **101:** Tatiana Kreminska/Alamy (ful sudani) ruizluquepaz/Getty Images (alfajores) Edalin Photography/ Shutterstock (whipped cream krumkake) Difydave/Getty Images Difydave/Getty Images Quanthem/Getty Images (lebkuchen); **104:** romiri/Shutterstock (tsitron) New Africa/Shutterstock (krinos ouzo); **105:** mama_mia/Shutterstock (gicopa candy) New Africa/Shutterstock (matgouel) Elena Schweitzer/Shutterstock (motiv zuckerl) Amy Lutz/Shutterstock (jolly rancher) studiomode/Alamy (candy fish); **106:** Emilio100/Shutterstock (chupa chups) SiljeAO/Shutterstock (vero mango) francis elzingre/Alamy (pierrot gourmand); **107:** David Esser/Shutterstock (nimm2 lizaki) Lenscap Photography/Shutterstock (dip dab) nick barounis/Alamy (tiger pops) SiljeAO/Shutterstock (look-o-look liquorice lollipops) Gevorg Simonyan/Shutterstock (melody pop); **109:** pius99/Getty Images (giza sphinx) Mulevich/Shutterstock (chupa chups) skodonnell/Getty Images (hershey's chocolate kiss) Eunjin Han/Shutterstock (gummy bear) Tanarch/Getty Images (cacao tree with cacao pods) benoitb/Getty Images (pez) Marc Bruxelle/Shutterstock (tire d'érable); **110:** Hayati Kayhan/Shutterstock (pistachio toffees) page frederique/Shutterstock (carambar caramels) GSDesign/Shutterstock (conos con cajeta) Keith Homan/Shutterstock (bon bons chewy candy); **111:** Rofidd/Shutterstock (torrone) Rofidd/Shutterstock (milky melon chews) Ho Su A Bi/Shutterstock (pineapple lumps) Nigel Wiggins/Shutterstock (fizzers) Pgiam/Getty Images (jelly beans) karacacennet/Shutterstock (turkish delight); **112:** Martin of Sweden/Shutterstock (julmust and butterscotch gummies) jirkaejc/Shutterstock (gummy sticks); **113:** MisterStock/Shutterstock (violet-flavored gummies) Edin fahmi/Shutterstock (gummi spicy mangos) Tobik/Shutterstock (gummy bears) manbo-photo/Getty Images (yuzu) D. Merrimon Crawford/Shutterstock (strawberry jellycious gummies); **114:** The Image Party/Shutterstock (dr. brown's cel-ray) magefingerprint/Shutterstock (mauby fizz); **115:** stephanhartmann/Getty Images (apfelschorle apple juice); **117**: Floortje/Getty Images (jellybeans) Keystone-France/Gamma-Keystone/Getty Images (candy store) Jennifer A Smith/Getty Images (jellybeans) rook76/Shutterstock (president ronald reagan) Aleksandr Dyskin/Shutterstock (parade) Pixel-Shot/Shutterstock (turkish delights); **118:** SiljeAO/Shutterstock (dark chocolate banana marshmallows) hendramgr/Shutterstock (kuhbonbon) vivooo/Shutterstock (jelly candies); **119:** vivooo/Shutterstock (souffle sweets) hendramgr/Shutterstock (kuhbonbon) Pixel-Shot/Shutterstock (pashmak) Manuta/Getty Images (marzipan); **120:** lovleah/Getty Images (violet crumble) radub85/Getty Images (kinder surprise eggs); **121:** NoirChocolate/Shutterstock (brigadeiro) Malcolm Haines/Alamy (milka bubbly) NeydtStock/Shutterstock (toblerone) corners74/Shutterstock (chocolate fish) Photoongraphy/Shutterstock (cacao); **122:** max blain/Shutterstock (musk sticks) philipreedphotography/Stockimo/Alamy (chicken bones); **123:** RMIKKA/ Shutterstock (salsagheti) Westend61 GmbH/SRS/Alamy (candied violets) Darya Lavinskaya/Shutterstock (ovos moles) Kenishirotie/Shutterstock (wagashi) philipreedphotography/Stockimo/Alamy (chicken bones)

127

For Abby and Andy, and for Jackson, whose curiosity and excitement about snacks around the world inspired this book. -Lisa M. Gerry

Author: Lisa M. Gerry
Editor: Priyanka Lamichhane
Illustrator: Toby Triumph
Designer: Ryan Hayes
Photo Editor: Alison O'Brien Muff
Publishing Director: Piers Pickard
Publisher: Rebecca Hunt
Art Director: Emily Dubin
Print Production: Nigel Longuet

Published in April 2025 by Lonely Planet Global Limited
CRN: 554153
ISBN: 9781837585762
www.lonelyplanet.com/kids
© Lonely Planet 2025
10 9 8 7 6 5 4 3 2 1
Printed in Malaysia

All rights reserved. No part of this publication may be reproduced, stored in a retrieval system or transmitted in any form by any means, electronic, mechanical, photocopying, recording or otherwise except brief extracts for the purpose of review, without the written permission of the publisher. Lonely Planet and the Lonely Planet logo are trademarks of Lonely Planet and are registered in the US Patent and Trademark Office and in other countries.

Although the author and Lonely Planet have taken all reasonable care in preparing this book, we make no warranty about the accuracy or completeness of its content and, to the maximum extent permitted, disclaim all liability from its use.

STAY IN TOUCH
lonelyplanet.com/contact

Lonely Planet Office:
IRELAND
Digital Depot, Roe Lane (off Thomas St), Digital Hub, Dublin 8, D08 TCV4, Ireland

MIX
Paper | Supporting responsible forestry
FSC™ C021741

Paper in this book is certified against the Forest Stewardship Council™ standards. FSC™ promotes environmentally responsible, socially beneficial and economically viable management of the world's forests.